Of What I Remember

A Novel By

Jazzlyn Unique Ingram

J.UNIQUE

PUBLISHED IT

Thank You

First, I would like to thank God for this opportunity. Thank you to my children. I am so proud to be your mommy. Thank you to my husband for living life with me and teaching me to have integrity. Thank you to my grandma for teaching me the importance of education and consistency. Thank you to my mom for teaching me to have faith in God. Thank you to my grandpa for teaching me how to pray and showing me what hard work means. Thank you to my uncle for showing me how to overcome life's obstacles. Thank you to my aunt for teaching me to be strong and always organized. Thank you to my siblings and cousins for teaching me to lead and loving me for me. Thank you to my father-in-law for teaching me the values of life. Thank you to my sisters from other misters. Y'all help me push to be the best version of me I can be. A special thank you to everyone who reads this novel.

This novel fictitiously describes the life of someone who has experienced quite a journey and is now healing through therapy. There is the use of real cities, places, and details of historic events that have occurred. This novel is to promote and encourage wellness. This book is in honor of Mental Health Awareness Month. While there is no official medical advice in this novel, the story promotes helping people be vulnerable, and ok with expressing their truths. "Health is wealth;" means more than just working out or money. Everyone must find ways to keep their life balanced in all areas. Like Whitley Gilbert-Wayne from *A Different World* would say, "Relax, Relate, Release!" LOL

Table of Contents

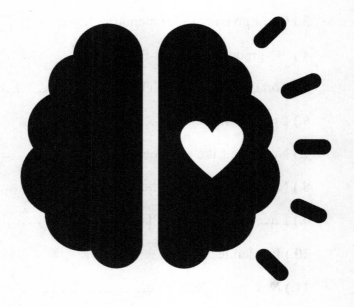

Take Care of your brain.
Your Mental Health Matters! - Jazz

CHAPTER 1

" Welcome to "We Care 4 U"

1

(Automatic Doors Open.)

(Automatic Doors Shut.)

(Automatic Doors Open.)

(Automatic Doors Shut.)

"Excuse Me!" says an elderly man, coughing harshly as he enters the building.

"Oh my god, I'm so Sorry!" Journee says startled, moving out of his way. She is standing in front of the "We Care 4 U" Health & Holistic Wellness Center. Journee is standing directly in front of the door sensor, triggering them to open and shut. However, she has yet to enter the building.

Today is Journee's first appointment with her new therapist. She takes a deep breath and finally enters the building...

The frigid air from the lobby was so overwhelming, it took her breath away. Despite the cold, her hands were clammy. Journee zips up her hoodie and continues down the hallway.

The sunlight was slowly fading as Journee progressed further into the dark building. Eventually all of the natural light disappeared, and florescent lighting blindingly took over. The building did not give good vibes. Journee thought to herself.

Journee began looking at signs, trying to figure out how to get to her appointment. There are multiple offices within this building. Signs for surgery point one way, a sign for pediatrics says go back outside. She did not have her glasses on, so she was over squinting at the signs. Journee decides she is going to reschedule for another day. As she turns to exit, a calm voice calls out to her.

"Can I Help you find something?" the voice says genuinely.

Journee turns towards the voice and a beautiful dark-skinned woman stood before her. Her almond shaped eyes, and bright smile glistened in the natural sunlight shining from the entrance. The woman is much taller than Journee.

She looks like a runway model. Her neon green scrubs are clean and pressed perfectly. Her scrubs are decorated with pins of achievements. She has a butterfly shaped pin that says, 10 years of service. Her badge says, Hospitality Manager: Ebony. Journee notices her lime green nails. They were a perfect coffin tip shape! Journee had a way of noticing things about people. Things many people don't pay attention to. Some call it nosey, but she genuinely enjoys observing everything around her.

"Yes, thank you. I am looking for the therapy department. I have an appointment with Dr. Stone." Journee says graciously, realizing that she is staring at Ebony.

"Of course. Follow me this way to the correct waiting area." Ebony says while gesturing to the right. Journee follows closely behind her.

After three turns, two hallways, and a small stairway, they finally reached the correct waiting room. In this room the fluorescent lights are competing with the natural sunlight. The brightly lit room had minimal décor. The walls are painted beige. The floors are as well.

There are portraits of diverse cultures of people hanging on the walls. A Hindu woman with a head covering, and a red dot in the middle of her forehead, is giving strong eye contact. The eye contact of all the images pierces through you. Another is a family that has albinism. Their fair skin and light hair is emphasized beautifully in the black and white image. The artist did a great job of capturing everyone's features.

Hard brown bucket chairs line the center and walls of the room. The room smelled sterile. Journee and Ebony passed two janitors mopping, so the overwhelming scent of bleach lingered.

The sounds of rain and nature is playing on the sound system. The speaker clearly had a short in it because the sound of static is giving the opposite of a calming vibe.

The room could seat at least thirty people. There are currently 7 people occupying various seats throughout the room. Some people acknowledge others when they enter the room, while others are avoiding eye contact at all costs. Journee was avoiding eye contact or at least trying to. One couple is having a conversation about topics less than appropriate for public areas.

There is glass surrounding the reception area for the staff's safety. It reminds Journee that staff views them as dangerous or a threat, and not someone seeking help. None of the other departments they walked past had glass barriers on their check-in desks. No one is currently occupying the receptionist's desk. Journee leans over to see the chart on the table. As she does, the same soft voice calls out to her again.

"Ok, you can sign in here on the kiosk and a nurse will call you up shortly. There are only a few people before you, so it should not be too long. If you need anything, here is a card with a QRC code to lead you to our website. There you will find lots of information and often asked questions. Good luck to you and have a wonderful day!" says Ebony as she walks away.

Journee was on her own again, and the anxiety was slowly rising. She checks in on the kiosk, pays her copay, and finds a seat near the window. Journee positions herself and her large bag, so that no one is welcome to sit in the seat beside her. At least she hopes. Some people are rude enough to still try to sit there. Sit right on her bag despite other seats being available.

Journee scrolls through her phone on social media. Her leg is shaking vigorously as she waits to hear her name called. The nurse keeps calling people back, but more people are steady filling the waiting room back up. She was happy she had an early appointment.

One man has been staring at Journee intensely since she sat down. She has tried to avoid eye contact, but because he has not broken his stare, it is impossible. He keeps flashing a gapped tooth smile at her in a sinister way. Right as Journee goes to ask him if he has a problem, she hears her name called out.

"Journee Ian!" A woman says loudly, standing at the entrance to the triage area. Journee waves her hand and says here, but the nurse does not hear her. Journee is sure she heard her, but she acts as if she didn't.

"Journee Hope Ian!" Shouted the nurse again, now sounding annoyed.

"I said here!" Journee snaps back just as loud. "Damn, tell everybody my entire government name." Journee says under her breath as she follows the nurse through the doors to the triage room.

"Excuse me?" The nurse says sarcastically, knowing Journee's statement was rhetorical.

"You heard me; but since you wanna bring it up. It is rude to yell out my full government name in a lobby full of strangers. The first two people you called, you only said their first name. Then the last person you called must be a regular because you made eye contact with them and SILENTLY gestured for them to come up. You need a consistent system for calling patients for their appointments. Keep us safe, like y'all protect yourselves. Your name tags only list your first names for a reason." Journee says annoyed, while reading **Nurse Leslie** off the woman's badge.

"Well, aren't you observant?" Nurse Leslie says in a sarcastic tone. "What is the big deal? These people don't know you or could care less about what you have going on. People are here to face bigger problems than your name sweetie." Nurse Leslie explains in a nice nasty tone.

(BING!)

Journee's phone notification rings loudly.

"See this is exactly what I am talking about." Journee turns her phone around for Nurse Leslie to see. On her screen is a friend request notification from the same creepy man that was staring at her in the lobby.

"I am going to block him; but now I have to be worried about another potential stalker. Also, no one found it weird that he was just sitting there. He was there before me and has yet to be called to the back." Journee says aggravated.

"I apologize." says Nurse Leslie, while acknowledging the profile photo is the same man from the lobby.

"I have never had anyone complain, nor show me they have been found online. I will bring this to my nurse managers attention at once." Nurse Leslie explains, flustered from being wrong.

"I appreciate your apology. It has happened before, so if I seem irritated, it is because with my name being so unique, they find me easily. I tried using nicknames, but social media updates enforced the use of my real name." Journee accepted the nurse's apology, but she is extremely uncomfortable and rethinking this entire process. Unfortunately for her it's mandatory.

Nurse Leslie's hands are shaking now. Her once dominant demeanor has crumbled, and if she drops her pen again, Journee is going to ask for another nurse.

Nurse Leslie manages to take Journee's vital signs and record her health history. She asks about Journee's educational history, sexual orientation, and sexual activity status. Nurse Leslie then asks about her family's health history. Next, she motions for Journee to step onto the scale. Journee could not see what her weight or sexual orientation had to do with her mental health. It only made her feel worse and judged.

Nurse Leslie has not said anything more than what was medically necessary since her awkward apology. Having egg on her face from being loud and wrong seems to have dampened her desire for small banter. She has stopped shaking and her facial expressions continuously show her displeasure with Journee's answers.

Noticing this, Journee decides to keep her answers brief. There is no point of telling this woman all of her business. She figured that she would have to explain all this again to the therapist. This is not her first time in therapy, but she is new to this facility. Over their interaction just as much as Journee, Nurse Leslie gestures for Journee to follow her to the therapy rooms.

"Doctor Stone will be in shortly to see you." Nurse Leslie manages to spit out, as she heads for the door. After their haphazard interaction she says, "I will be sure to make a report of the incident that occurred today. I apologize again." The door hits her as she quickly exits the room.

"That's a damn shame." Journee chuckles to herself. Journee has zero faith in Nurse Leslie's last statement. She knew that if she wanted to see change, she would have to report the incident herself. When the door closed, it closed tightly. Silencing the sounds of the hallway immediately. The only sound you can hear is the air blowing slowly from the a/c unit. That makes sense because people are here to discuss private topics. However, it causes Journee's anxiety to rise.

Journee is analyzing every angle of the room. She notices that the room is colorfully decorated, more so than the waiting area. There is a picture of a family on the desk. A man, a woman, and three small children gaze back at Journee. She sees herself in the reflection of the frame. She finds herself beginning to fight back tears as the door swings open. Another figure appears in the photo's reflection. Journee quickly goes to place the photo back down on the desk and drops it just shy of the desktop. It falls to the floor in a manner that feels like its moving in slow motion, until it crashes loudly on the floor.

The thick shards of glass shatter across the floor in front of the desk. Journee and the person in the reflection jump back. However, Journee swiftly steps forward to clean up her mistake.

"I am so sorry!" Journee says quickly, kneeling to grab the glassless photo and frame. Before she can reach to pick it the person in the reflection grabs her arm.

Journee quickly pulls away but notices a series of scars on the arm grabbing towards her. The scars are accompanied by an array of delicate tattoos. Pastel colored tulips, monarch butterflies, and a tattoo of what appears to be a signature that reads, *"Stone to Stone"* lay perfectly around the keloid raised skin. Journee always notices people that have tattoos, because she has them and understands they can be symbolic to a person. She also notices when people don't have tattoos. They immediately are uniquely interesting to her. Some of those people judge, but some desire ink and just did not get the opportunity to get them.

"I apologize for touching your arm, but please don't touch the glass with your bare hands." A woman says in a warm tone. "I am Dr. Stone. I will go grab a broom and be right back. I can see it on your face that you feel bad, but I promise it's ok. It was a mistake. It's not like you broke my family up, just the frame." Dr. Stone says with a chuckle hoping to cheer Journee up.

Journee, still uneasy, is unable to muster up a forced laugh at this moment. Her stomach is in knots, and she is ready to be home like yesterday. Dr. Stone's efforts did not work, so she goes on with the session.

"Oh-kay, you can take a seat anywhere you like. I will be right back." Dr. Stone states, exiting the room.

There is more than one option available for Journee to choose to sit. She notices a line of rainbow-colored bean bags against the wall first. Then she noticed an old green sofa that had *That '70s show* written all over it.

There is a large cherry oak desk and rolling chair. That is obviously Dr. Stone's desk. Journee was going to be sarcastic and sit in Dr. Stone's seat; until she notices a small sign that says, **"Yes, you can sit here too!** Well, it's not funny if you have permission, Journee thought to herself. She decides to sit on the sofa near the window. The green color made her nauseous, but the view outside was beautiful

There is a flowing stone river path; weaved through a perfectly manicured green lawn. There is a large elephant statue sitting in the center of the fountain. It's trunk is pointing up and spraying water into the air. There are pastel-colored flowers strung along the path in pots hanging. They connect colorfully painted lamp posts that line the path. The facility sat nestled between a country club and a private school academy. It all looked like a dream to Journee. The trail had white gazebos spaced out along the path. People are sitting and enjoying the scenery. It is a warm Spring day in North Carolina and the bees are out.

"OK. Let's get this cleaned up so we can get started." Dr. Stone says coming back into the room to sweep up the debris. She places her now glassless family photo back onto her desk.

"Would you believe me if I told you that is not the first time this frame has dropped?" Dr. Stone says while walking to her desk. Journee continues to stare out the window, unaware Dr. Stone not only returned to the room, but was speaking to her.

"Well, let's get started shall we?" Dr. Stone says cheerfully, despite Journee's standoffish reception.

"As I stated before, I am Dr. Stone. You can call me Alesha. I will be completing your intake today. An intake appointment usually lasts about three to four hours. If we need a second session, we can schedule one. However, our goal is to get you placed with the Provider that best fits you. We will also discuss medication therapy. Medicines may help with any symptoms you may be experiencing, like fatigue and anxiety. Medication is not mandatory. If you start a routine it can always be reevaluated and adjusted.

Ok, let's see. During the next step of the intake, I will ask you a series of questions. I also will leave room for you to share your story. Based on your order of events and needs, we will design a treatment plan for you that blends medical and holistic practices. How does that sound? Any questions so far?" Dr. Stone smiles warmly at Journee.

"No." Journee says simply. Her leg has not stopped shaking since she sat down on the sofa. She is not feeling her normal talkative self. She is still thinking about the man in the lobby and how rude Nurse Leslie was to her.

"Ok, if at any time you have a question, or you want to go over something we can. If you need to vent or feel that you are losing grasp on life in any way, please bring it to your providers attention immediately. We listen and we don't judge here! You can speak freely. This is a safe space to heal. I have heard it all. From people of all different walks of life. You can curse or speak freely about your sexual experiences. We can discuss positive and negative moments from your life. The objective is to heal from trauma, but I enjoy hearing moments from your life that were not traumatic as well. It makes me happy to know that my patients have joy in their lives.

Alright, I am going to begin by telling you a little about myself. I like to start with my backstory and why I became a psychiatrist." Dr. Stone goes to speak, and Journee rudely cuts her off.

"Let me tell the story for you. From the looks of the picture I dropped and all of these degrees on the wall; you grew up in the country in a huge farmhouse. Your Mom and Dad were middle to upper class and pushed you to be the best version of you that you can be. You graduated top of your class, a virgin." Journee chuckles and continues her rant.

"You fall in love in college with a band or tech geek. Y'all graduated and had three beautiful kids together. You probably live in Cary and just love helping "people like me." Did I get it right?"

"Well, no not completely. You did not get it all right. Whilst I did graduate top of my class." Dr. Stone says with immense pride. "I did not grow up in the country. I am from the slums of Washington, DC. I was found in a trash can, behind a roach infested motel. My birth mother and her "trick," were both found dead in their room from a drug overdose the same day.

My adoptive parents raised me from then on. I was raised in a middle-class neighborhood and taught the importance of education for sure. I am extremely grateful for them. My birth mother was a prostitute and on drugs her entire pregnancy. She did not know she was pregnant let alone who my father was. The doctors say I am a miracle. By the Grace of God, I made it."

Journee's leg stops shaking and she leans forward as Dr. Stone continues her story.

"I could not have graduated as a virgin, because I was pregnant in my junior year of high school. I dropped out and married my boyfriend who was 10 years older than me. He lived an extremely dangerous lifestyle. He got a hold of laced drugs, and it sent him into a rage. He tried to kill me and our son. He shot us. Thank God, we survived. He did not. The bullet from the gunshot wound he gave himself made me a widow." Dr. Stone takes a pause and then smiles again as she continues her story.

"The man in the photo is my new husband. We did meet in college because I went back to school. I got my GED first. Then I met him in Community College. Society can make people feel ashamed to go back to school, but it was the best decision I ever made. That is why I became a Psychiatrist. To help people before it gets to that point. If we are paying attention to those around us, and living intentionally, we can avoid losing someone because we realized they needed help "too late." We all face struggles. No two people will bounce back the same from trauma. Everyone has to cope and adapt to heal. If we pray, plan, and prepare, we can overcome anything." Dr. Stone finishes her statement and awaits Journee's response.

"I am so Sor..." Journee goes to apologize, but Dr. Stone stops her.

"Please do not apologize. There is no way you could have known what I have been through. I pride myself on not looking like what I have been through, with the exception of my scars. I wear these as a badge of honor that I am still here. I overcame it all with God's grace and mercy." Dr. Stone says genuinely.

Journee had a lump in her throat and was holding back tears again. She could not believe that she had judged Dr. Stone so harshly. She hated when people did the same thing to her; so why was it ok for her to do? It wasn't. Journee felt like a hypocrite.

"You do not have to be sad for me. God has been very good to me. I am here. That is why I said you can call me Alesha. I share my story, so you know that I am human. I am not just a professional title. I've had to overcome struggles. I had a rough start and then God blessed me with my parents. I made many decisions; and now I have to walk the path that those decisions placed me on. I had to go on my own healing journey. It was not easy, but I learned so many things that saved my life and others along the way. I have acquired a set of skills that will help you keep going in some of the darkest valleys. Starting with *Psalms 23*, I say that anytime I feel weary in a situation." Dr. Stone says serenely.

Journee could not believe the words Dr. Stone chose to use. Her motto in life is Keep Going, no matter what you're faced with. Like the Late Great Reverend Dr. Martin Luther King Jr. said,"

"If you can't fly then run, if you can't run then walk, if you can't walk then crawl, but whatever you do, you have to keep moving forward."

Journee also noticed what Dr. Stone, Alesha said about God. Journee's faith is something that she takes very seriously.

She feels so much better about talking to Alesha, but she feels horrible about how she has been acting. Journee begins to tear up again. Dr. Stone hands her a napkin.

"Breathe deeply with me." Dr. Stone leads by taking a long deep breath in and exhaling slowly.

"I like to take deep breaths often, just so you know. I am glad to see it says you do yoga. Meditation is great for your health. Take your time and we can begin the process of speaking about you; when you're ready!" Dr. Stone says warmly.

CHAPTER 2

"The Early Years"

2

Journee takes a moment to gather herself, after hearing Dr. Stone's story about her life. She knows what she shared can only be a glimpse into what she has been through. Journee feels honored that Alesha felt comfortable to share. That was a first for her. Most therapists made her feel judged or misunderstood.

"Ok, what do you want to know? I mean, where should I start?" Journee says taking a deep breath.

"Let me explain the process." Dr. Stone says with a smile

"As you know, a mandatory requirement of your post incarceration probationary period is to complete this program. The mandatory portion of the program lasts 6 months. However, we decided to take the program a step further. Your first 6 months will satisfy your requirements for probation. If you choose to accept the full treatment plan, it is a long term program that is adjusted to your specific needs. Everyone starts at the same step, which is Intake. The program is called "Timeline Therapy." Timeline Therapy is an intensive healing program. You may discuss anything with your provider. The goal is to heal from past traumas, not just because you were incarcerated. Life gives challenges to everyone, but not everyone is taught how to manage and cope with those challenges.

I created this program to help providers and patients go deep beneath the surface, and in chronological order of events. We do not want to overstimulate you or cause anxiety. However, we do want to pinpoint any triggers or patterns in your behaviors. Also evaluating how you learn or face everyday tasks. Learning these things about yourself can help you manage your emotional reactions when faced with a challenge.

In traditional therapy you can discuss the past, present, or future in any order, and remain on one topic. There may not be a system in place to target that specific experience, or a program to help with future planning. Any form of therapy is a phenomenal step in the right direction. We have our own unique way of doing things. Many people have found great success participating in this program. This program was designed to go in order from your earliest memory to

24

current events. Each session will consist of a one-hour block. You must have at least one session a month, but you can do weekly or biweekly if you desire.

The sessions will go in order based on the timeline we create today. Each period of your life can have a maximum of five sessions, with each session being an hour long. Once we reach current day, you should have had the opportunity to face any unresolved trauma from your past. Then we leave it in the past. We will never forget, and that's a balance in life. A lot of people wish they did not have to remember a bad experience. However, taking away the bad memories removes the good memories as well. We let go and let God. Our shortcomings do not dictate our opportunity to try again. Does that sound like something you would be prepared to participate in?"

"Yes I am willing to participate in the extended program. I understand this intake is to make a timeline of what I remember about my life…" Journee says as her mind begins to race through experiences.

"Ok! That is great to hear. This is a decision made for you. Others will benefit from your growth, change, and improvements. However, this has to be a choice made for you. Your motivation or what drives you cannot be to satisfy outside or others, because if those variables change, you may run the risk of losing your identity.

Be ok with being authentically yourself, no matter who is around. Especially when you are alone. Those times with just you, and God, have to be prioritized. You need moments of calm to reflect and plan. Ok, let us continue with the steps of the program and more of what to expect.

I designed a notebook for the provider to record your story, and a healing journal for you that has healing activities, journal pages, and recipes for mental health support! There is a page for today's intake. The provider uses their notebook to jot down key words or pertinent information about a specific time period or traumatic event.

I always explain this part in depth because I do not want anyone to feel while their provider is taking notes, that they are not paying attention. We record the information and try our best to be descriptive, to curate a program that will guide you best on your healing journey. Are you ok with the process so far?" Dr. Stone says as she begins writing Journee's name on the notebook assigned to her.

Journee hated that there would be a notebook of all her personal moments. Then she realized what is written online about her, so talking to Dr. Stone can't be that bad.

"I appreciate you explaining this. What is the likelihood that I end up with you as my therapist, and what happens to the notebook when we finish?" Journee says flipping through the colorful healing journal gifted to her.

"That is a great question. I was going to tell you at the end of our session, but I will tell you now. I have one opening left for the year on my books, and I would like to offer it to you. The program is covered by your insurance. We are meshing well, and I do not want to place you with a male provider. I see you listed female as your preference, and males are all I have available at this time.

As for the notebook, once you complete the program, you get to keep it. You keep your healing journal of course as well. As we go along today you can write on the section that says intake. Its blank for you to write whatever you like. Notes about what you tell me, questions, or events that you may want to target for deeper healing.

As you go along in the program the pages have a spot for the date, therapist name, which would be me, and the period you are discussing each session.

There is a wrap up page for after each session. That is for important notes or homework that you are assigned. Before you worry, know the only homework is to write a journal entry at home. There is a journal page for you after each session sheet. Do You have any questions before we begin? Oh! There are drinks available in the mini fridge. You can help yourself to those and snacks while we talk." Dr. Stone says warmly.

Journee notices the snack display beautifully arranged above the fridge. The vibes are much better here than the entrance of the building or waiting area.

"Ok thank you, and yes I am ready to begin…" Journee says, still uncertain where all of this would lead.

Dr. Stone looks over Journee's paperwork file.

"Ok, I see here that you have been married for 14 years and have two children. I see that you have an extensive medical and mental health history. I see you suffered several miscarriages. I apologize for your losses. It says here that you were born in 1989. Let's start your timeline.

You can speak about where you are from. We will discuss your earliest memories, good or bad. We start with toddler to fifth grade. Middle school is the next period we will discuss. Then High school. Next, the college age years and transitioning to adulthood. We will then discuss your relationships, prior and leading up to your marriage. That can include discussing children, finances, any infidelities, and loss. Then you may discuss your incarceration period, and what led to your arrest. Lastly, we will wrap up on current feelings and events.

We also have additional programs for life planning, nutrition/ weight management, and manifestation. They meet once a month, and they make vision boards and Charcuterie boards! I will give you all of that information at the end of our session today.

Ok, if I stop you at any time, I am not being rude. I may need clarity or time to write. I may also have tips and coping skills to share with you. You can begin whenever you are ready."

"Ok, well I came busting out my momma's big...ha-ha never mind." Journee says laughing to herself.

"Coochie." says Dr. Stone with a slight grin on her face.

Journee looked up in shock. She was not sure what was more shocking. The fact that Dr. Stone said "coochie," or that she knew the book she was referencing.

"What? You didn't think I knew Sister Souljah? I love *The Coldest Winter Ever*. Have you read her newest novel *Love After Midnight*?" Dr. Stone says with passion.

Journee was shocked. Not only did Dr. Stone, Alesha, know her favorite author, but she even knew a book that she had not read yet.

"No, I will have to look that one up. I read *Midnight*!" Journee says putting a note in her phone to buy the book.

"Oh yes that is a great read as well, but she has titles since then that are great, check them out for sure!

I love her and Toni Morrison. *Song of Solomon* is one of my favorites. I have a small library here of books for patients to borrow, and if there is a book that's specific to your process; I will gift it to you."

Journee notices two white bookshelves sitting in the corners behind the desk area. There are books of all colors and sizes.

"I love *Dr. Maya Angelou.* Ah Ha that's it. I can say that is one of my earliest memories. My grandma kept bookshelves full of books and is an avid reader. My older cousin was an avid reader as well. Ever since we were kids I remember seeing her with a book. The cover of *Flyy Girl by Omar Tyree* always caught my attention, and *Terry McMillan* books. She kept several books by Author Gwen Byrd. My favorite is Jitterbug Jimmy. I would look at the books for fun, and as I learned to read them, I traveled through time often."

"I love that you referenced reading as time traveling. That is a fantastic way of looking at. I love to read. Please continue." Dr. Stone interjects.

"Um. I am originally from Rochester, New York. It is in upstate New York, not New York City. I specify because some people don't know there is a difference. I have been to NYC many times though. My mom allowed me to model as a child. I loved dressing up. I loved going on auditions and being on set. I was featured on a few commercials and ads. My favorite was for the *Kodak Marquee* Billboard in *Times Square*." Journee says reminiscing.

"I have been to Rochester before. I have family and friends that live in Buffalo. I love garbage plates! I have family in Brooklyn as well. You mentioned your grandma. Did you spend time with her often?" Dr. Stone says cheerfully.

Journee was beginning to think this was too good to be true. Alesha knew where she was from and had even been there. Journee knew she was not lying because it is IYKYK when it comes to a garbage plate. This made Journee feel safe; to let her guard down a bit and continue with the session.

"Yes, my grandma raised me. I lived with her, my uncle, and cousin. I lived with my mom and my siblings at times. My mom always stayed close to my grandma to help with my uncle. My Grandpa would come to help my uncle who is paralyzed. I have an aunt and cousins who visited us on weekends and summer breaks. I had a nanny who cared for me in early childhood as well. She was amazing. My grandma had a friend that helped us over the years as well. She helped me understand things about myself. She kept a short cut, but I think of her every time I brush my hair. She taught me to start at the ends, and gently comb through to the roots, so I didn't rip my hair out! I am grateful for all of them.

"What about your father? Did you spend time with him often?" Dr. Stone asks while writing in her notebook.

"I feel like Bruce the Shark from *Finding Nemo*, I never knew my father, but it's true." Journee says with a chuckle.

"My mom was a teenager when she had me. I will say this now though, I come from women who may have had their children young, but they took care of us and their responsibilities well. My mom was just getting her life going and I said hello! She met my dad at her job. They dated, but she decided to move back to New York. She headed back home not knowing I was in her belly! When I was old enough she told me his name and where he was from.

I can remember when having a computer in your house became a common thing.

I would sit for hours trying to find his name online, but I failed to ever find a match. I took a DNA test and did not find any matches. I eventually gave up. I had to realize I made it through each day without him, and like *Boys II Men* said I am doing just fine. He probably doesn't even know I exist. My mom was always present in my life. Even if she had to leave she would find ways to leave a piece of her. Every Valentine's Day she would buy me the bears with the year on the foot. If she did not hand it to me directly, she would leave it on my bed. She would take me with her to get her "iridescent cotton candy" nails done. Then we would get *Taco Bell*. She was good at making Banana Pudding too!

She is so smart. Besides looking just like her, I take after her love of learning and valuing education. I cannot spell anything wrong on a project or flyer; she proofreads and corrects everything. You better not "AXE" her for anything but ASK ha-ha." Journee chuckles to herself again.

"HAHA I can relate to that one. My parents were the same way when I was growing up. Sorry, Please continue." Dr. Stone says laughing.

"She got it from my grandma because she takes school very seriously. She made it fun to learn and was always willing to help. It was important to do well in school. My grandma is from the south. She got her education while dealing with uncertain times, racism, and disrespect. She lost both her parents and grandparents before she was 13 years old. She had my aunt at 15 years old, my mom two years later, and my uncle 3 years after that. She relocated to New York and had to learn things on her own. She helped us understand why it is important to appreciate the opportunities we have. She did an excellent job taking care of us.

I was born two years after my uncle had an accident that left him paralyzed. They loved and watched my uncle walk for 15 years and that abruptly changed. My grandma gets sad every time she hears *Luther Vandross's* song, *Since I Lost My Baby*. It reminds her of her baby becoming paralyzed. He beats the odds every day and is still fighting strong!" Journee takes a deep breath and prepares to continue her story.

Dr. Stone briefly interjects.

"I am going to pause you for a moment, because you addressed some key points that I would like to discuss. I noticed that you make jokes about things that may cause others pain. That is a common coping mechanism for people who have experienced great trauma. Or even uncontrollable laughter in moments that are considered inappropriate. That is a nervous response. I am in no way judging you, it is just an observation. I heard you say eventually you gave up on your father. I want you to know that it is ok to be sad, angry, confused, or feel a void in his absence.

I know people who say you cannot miss something you never had. When it comes to parents, I always acknowledge that everyone has two. There are yearly reminders to celebrate your parents, so even when you try not to think about it. It is still possible for something to trigger those emotions. I feel that knowing where you come from has an influence on your development and how you manage life. Even if you do not meet the people who made you, it is still important to know. So, I do not want you to just brush those feelings to the side. We will go more in depth in future sessions about this, but I wanted to pinpoint that statement.

I also wanted to address the injury that your uncle sustained. I apologize for the pain he must have endured and your family having to support him after such a tragedy. It is very honorable of your family for choosing to care for him in the home. So often I see patients whose families have left them in group homes. We will discuss that as well and what that environment was like in a later session. But this is valuable information. Please continue."

"Thank you for that. We refer to my uncle as our Job, like the bible, because despite his injuries, his faith is stronger than anyone I know. If you ask him how he is, he will tell you blessed! I appreciate what you said about my dad. I have had thirty-five plus years to heal and accept life without a father. I love my mom and appreciate that she kept me with family. She could have gotten rid of me. She could have given me away. I have friends who come from adoption or foster care. We are all thankful to be loved.

Our relationship has been a rollercoaster. It is because we have the same zodiac sign. I am her child for sure! We both are enthusiastic and love Mariah Carey Ha-Ha! I learned to let her speak and then message her later to say how I felt. I hate arguing and yelling with her. Most times it is a misunderstanding, but it sounds like all-out war. I am grateful we are in a better place these days. The teenage years were rough, like any other mom and daughters' story of coming of age.

I will say overall from my earliest memory to fifth grade that life was cool and full of adventure. My mom had my room decorated with colorful signs and educational posters. My grandma loved to be outside. We rode bikes and rollerbladed at *Genesee Valley Park*. I loved playing at *Manhattan Square Park*, & the ice skating rink. She would garden in our backyard. She was a mail carrier and everywhere we went someone knew her and had to speak.

I loved seeing how happy people would be to see her. I knew that meant she was good to people. She took pride and cared about her job. She would take me to the Big Man store on Hudson Ave to get ketchup chips and snacks. The giant statue of the man is gone, but I still go to that store when I go home. She loved going to the Public Market. We would get fresh fruit like plums and nectarines.

We ate a lot of vegetables too. She would let me get empanadas at the vendors. My favorite would be to get a fish fry from *Captain Jim's* on main street.

38

A good part of my childhood we were pescatarians and only ate fish. When we weren't, we loved going to *G&G Steakout*. The original one, that was on the corner of Hudson Ave and North Street. Near the *S & T Lounge*. I heard *G&G Steakout* is back. I will have to try it next time I am home. I have not had anything as good as the original ones to date!" Journee chuckles.

"I know exactly what you're talking about. I have had one of those subs and that sauce and how it's made is one of a kind for sure! Please continue." Dr. Stone says reminiscing.

"We went to church growing up. We went to *Zion Hill Missionary Baptist Church*. Our family went there for years. I would often go with my grandma and mom, but at times I went with my uncle and grandpa. I learned at an early age all churches are different. I loved singing in the choir and being an usher. We changed to a new church over the years. Our family was very involved in church. I loved watching my aunt draped in her African gowns read the announcements or deliver the sermon. Watching her is where my passion for public speaking began. I loved going to bible study and getting to eat after too!" Journee chuckles.

"My elementary school did a lesson that included trips to different churches. I think schools should still offer this activity. We went to different types of churches, to experience each other's cultures and beliefs. I got to wear a hijab when we went to the Islamic mosque. I learned Hebrew at the Jewish temple, and got to see a Catholic confession room after Mass. All those moments shaped how I viewed others, and walking in their shoes. I try my best not to judge."

"That's right, we listen, and we do not judge! Please continue." says Dr. Stone smiling.

"Exactly, Ha-Ha! Well, the nanny that I referenced earlier would keep me during the day at her home. She lived in Rochester's *19th ward* on a little side street that felt like a fantasy world. She kept a garden and an exceptionally clean home. She would let me nap and then we would eat and play outside. She let me play with the girl next door until she used bad language and that was the end of that.

She did not tolerate disrespect. She was a kind and elegant woman. She would let me play and dress up with her clothes and jewelry. I loved helping her in the kitchen. We would walk and take the *RTS* bus. She explained to me who *Rosa Parks* was, and the significance of being able to sit anywhere on the bus. My favorite place she took me was *Midtown Plaza*. It was so beautiful during the holiday season. There was a display of clocks from around the world and a train that went around the mall. That area is so different now, but I heard they recently restored the clocks. I cannot wait to go home and see them.

As I got older, I did gymnastics at *Bright Raven Gymnastics Center*. I started going to summer camp. I eventually was playing sports. I played soccer and basketball. I ran track. I jumped hurdles and threw discus.

I love spending time with my family. My grandpa would cut grass, while my grandma would garden. My grandpa loves bowling; I got to go a few times. I loved playing in the arcade! He would take my uncle and I, to *Greece Ridge Mall*. I loved when the RVs were there. I would go on them and describe the inside to my uncle, because he could not get in them. He always wanted one. I wish we had phones back then, like we do now. I would have been able to take a video and show him. I am trying to figure out how to get a handicap accessible RV for him now! We would go fishing at the park. I would just watch and listen to my cd player. I did not like worms!

I loved going to the *YMCA*. I went to a program out past my house for years. I learned arts and crafts and how to boondoggle. We would tie dye shirts and have slip & slide competitions.

We had pizza parties and took trips to the ice cream shops. They took us on field trips every week. They would take us to *Seneca Park Zoo*, *The Strong Museum*, The Planetarium, and the movie theater. I have been canoeing on *Braddock Bay*. They would take us to swim and build sandcastles on Hamlin and Charlotte Beaches. I have been hiking and swimming at *Letchworth State Park* and *Stoney Brook State Park*. I loved going to the amusement parks. *Seabreeze* and *Six Flags Darien Lake* were the highlights of every summer for me. I could not wait to be a teenager to walk around with my boyfriend one day. I was in such a rush to grow up. I know now why my grandma would say,"

"Take your time! Don't be in a rush to grow up. You will be an adult longer than you will be a child."

"She was right. I eventually changed to the program downtown. I did not stay in that camp long though, because they opened a new program near our house. I finished attending as a CIT (counselor in training) when I was 13.

I learned how to be explorative and independent over the years of going to camp. I am so grateful to my mom and grandma for allowing me to go. I did not have many issues while at camp. My older cousin that lived with me went to summer camp for a while and then he stopped going. He is much older than me and was normally in his own world. I spent time with his siblings aka my cousins on weekends and summers.

We all got along, but like kids we had our quarrels. They picked on me for being an only child at the time and being a crybaby. I was a bit emotional at times, but I meant well. I loved hanging out with my aunt. We went to the mall, the zoo, and her house was dope. She was fashionable and fun. She was no nonsense though. If you do not do as she asks, that's your ass! She kept her house exceptionally clean and organized as well. I learned from all of them to clean my home!" Journee smiles and pauses for a moment.

"I have not had to stop you because all the information you are giving me is the foundation of who you are. Those memories are what shaped your perspective of not only how you grew up; but that was the beginning of manifesting the life that you are living now. Where you developed morals and beliefs. Manners and mannerisms. I do not want to push you into any areas, but I would like to open a space for you to discuss any areas of trauma from childhood you would like to address?" Dr. Stone says warmly.

"We would take trips to visit family in Virginia and D.C. In Virginia there were more boy cousins than girl cousins to play with. Because of that they kept me in the house close to them. An incident occurred when we were young, that ruined my chances of being out of sight.

While playing house and driving in our fake car, I was the mom and my other cousin, the dad. He said I had to kiss him, so I kissed his cheek. The younger cousin in the back seat wanted a kiss as well. When I declined, he went crying up the stairs. He said I kissed the other cousin and would not kiss him. All they heard was kiss and it was over. No more playing.

They said I ruined trips for them. They hated having to check for me and me always asking to play. I feel bad because I genuinely wanted to play, but I do not blame them looking back. Kids need to learn proper behavior and be watched. Sad thing is what they tried to avoid still happened.

We were on a trip visiting family. Another one of my boy cousins was sleeping over. I was sleeping on the floor next to him and my grandma was sleeping on the sofa. He whispered for me to come closer to him in the dark. He went on to touch and lick my vagina. As he went to do it again my grandma woke up on the sofa and called for me to get back closer to her.

That was it for that trip, but he would make more moments later in life. It introduced me to physical and nonconsensual touch. To be honest it made me curious; despite learning in that moment, based on her reaction that it was wrong." Journee says with her leg shaking again.

"Ok, I am going to pause you here. I would like you to take a deep breath with me. I noticed that your leg began to shake again. That is ok and a normal response when discussing things that make us uncomfortable. I am proud of you for saying the challenging things and facing your truths. I would like for us to pause for a moment and stand up with me. I would like you to reach for the ceiling and then reach to your toes. Taking deep breaths the entire time.

Inhale... Exhale..." Dr. Stone says gesturing her instructions.

Journee Stands and does the stretching exercise. The deep breathing helped more than she could have imagined. She then grabs a bottle of water out of the fridge and sits back down.

"I wanted to take a moment to stretch and reset. I am glad that you got something to drink. Now I can! I always wait for patients to drink or have a snack first. You held out on me ha-ha." Dr. Stone attempts to joke, but notices Journee's leg is still shaking. "You can continue telling me about this period of your life."

"Ok, well second to fourth grade were normal enough. I went to catholic school for kindergarten, a different catholic school for first grade and then to public school for second grade to ninth grade. I was ok with the other students. I did well in class, but my teachers did say I struggled to sit still and would talk out of turn.

My mom met a man and had fallen in love. They had a whirlwind romance. I could see how happy she was. She graduated from school and my little sister came into this world. Her dad was kind to me, and his family was as well. I was so excited to have a sibling. She was so cute as a baby.

As she got older we discussed that she felt I was mean to her when we were younger. That hurt me to hear because I thought I was very loving towards her. I of course did not like when she messed my stuff up, but I love her always. I do not think she understood the significant difference of being a 15 year old girl, working, going to school, and being in a relationship, and her being 8 years old.

I was stressed and she was that and would come to hug me, but I needed space sometimes. I will never ignore her or her feelings and will always be there for her. I acknowledged her feelings during our conversation and let her know that I never intended for her to feel disregarded. I am so glad she was able to articulate to me how she felt, and we are great now! She is the best auntie!

My mom and her dad's relationship unfortunately did not stay the same, and they decided to be co parents. My sister would have to spend time away and then with us. I know she would have fun, but I hated it when she left. My mom did not date and stayed to herself for years. Then she met a man that would change our lives forever." Journee says looking out the window again.

"I appreciate you sharing your story thus far. It sounds like you had an amazing childhood. I am saddened to hear that you experienced the moment with your cousin. It is possible he was reenacting something that he saw. You both were very young and impressionable. Children are curious. They are exploring and learning themselves. To be honest adults are too.

We all are trying to find the balance in life. A good balance is to learn from the past and those who came before us. We must work hard in the present to invent great things. Doing this will improve our way of living now and provide a better future for those to come tomorrow. Please continue." Dr. Stone says serenely.

"That is a beautiful perspective. I definitely pray to see that become our reality, and touch and agree with you. Well, I was explaining that my mom met a man. I was in elementary school when they met. He was a real charmer. I will never forget, my cousin and I were looking out the window. He pulled up in a limo to pick my mom up for their date. My cousin says aloud…"

"OOOH Journee that's your new dad?!"

"I looked at her crazy and said that is not my dad. I did not know then why I was suddenly so uncomfortable. I was so happy for my mom, but I also did not want to move away from my grandma and uncle. I had to leave them…

We started spending more nights at his house. He lived in a nice neighborhood. It was on the other side of the city and because of it I would be late for school. The teachers chose to make an example of me when I arrived. I had to enter at the top of the hallway and pass all the other classrooms to get to mine. They would stop speaking and stare or say things like, "this is getting ridiculous Journee." I hated it because it was not like I drove myself." Journee pauses with a wrinkled brow.

"That was not a burden that should have been laid on you. Whilst I am sure there were reasons your mom was running behind, it was up to them to address her if necessary to speak of it to anyone. You also do that in a private manner. You do not want to embarrass the student. I also wanted to say that it was normal for you to be uncomfortable.

Change is hard. Especially because you experienced a relationship with your sister's dad and that ended. It was completely normal for you to feel how you felt. If anything, it showed how emotionally intelligent you were at an early age. You were thinking on a deeper level than most children around that age. Your environment molds your behaviors of course. In good and bad ways.

Your uncle being in a wheelchair is one example of that. I know that you have witnessed things that many have not living with him, but please continue." Dr. Stone says preparing to write.

"Thank you, and yes it was quite an experience. It made all of us stronger and stand on our faith.

Ok, back to "stepdad." He drove a nice car. It had peanut butter leather seats, and it always smelled clean. Everything of his smelled slightly like his cologne. He was smart and had accomplished a lot for himself as a black entrepreneur. He was a real life prince charming.

He took us to church with his family. He took us on trips. One time he took us to Philly to try authentic cheesesteaks. I am a sliced cheese over whiz girl, but it was an enjoyable experience. It all seemed good until the good was gone...

Things started to take a turn. They did not argue often, but when they did disagree you could feel the tension. I learned how to deal with conflict in my relationships from my mom.

That is good in some ways, and I had to improve my behaviors in other ways. I love that she taught me to keep a clean home, and when you go in public to be presentable. I had to learn that everything does not need to be yelled. Haha! Things changed gradually. He wanted to be in control of everything. He wanted me to call him dad, and I was not ready to do so. I wanted to get comfortable, but it felt too soon. He took me shopping and brought me my first pair of brand name sneakers. My family did not allow me to wear certain brands. He told me to work hard to have nice things and to take care of myself.

Back at the house I would give him massages on his knees and back. He had injuries from college sports. It seemed innocent until it was not. I was at the house with him by myself. He said another family member was coming over too, but they "cancelled." I gave him a massage as I always did, but when I finished, he said…"

"OK, it's your turn!"

"I declined but he insisted. I reluctantly laid on my stomach on the ground of the living room. I can remember the room feeling cold and it was dark outside, because the streetlights were on. He had never given me a massage when my mom was home. He went on to massage my calves slowly. He massaged the back of my legs. He then massaged the inside of my thighs and finally, he touched my vagina. I flinched thinking it was a mistake. The way his fingers slid around the second time I knew it was no mistake. That is where my chest gets tight, and the memory gets dark." Journee says shaking her leg aggressively now.

"He came back later in life… I will tell you about that when we get to that period of the timeline. I naturally began to be disrespectful towards him. I cannot explain where it would come from. I refused to call him dad, and I hated everything he did. I hated how he chewed. I no longer saw him as a hero. Thankfully, I moved back in with my grandma."

"Journee, I would like for you to take a deep breath with me again." Dr. Stone leads Journee in two deep breaths. "I understand that talking about certain memories and traumas can be overwhelming. The point of all of this is not just to stir up old emotions, but to truly plan to heal and live a life free of anxiety. To be freed from the chains of our past. I want you to know that you are brave in facing yourself and these experiences.

As common as it is, and I hate to say that it is more common than people want to admit. Wrong is wrong, and that was wrong. It was not ok. He should not have touched you in that way. I apologize you were in the care of someone you were supposed to be able to trust, and they betrayed your trust." Dr. Stone says empathetically.

Journee begins fighting back tears.

"I look forward to going deeper in another session about that part of my life. I still have a lot of resentment towards that situation."

"That is completely understandable, and I have put a star next to this note. We will go deeper in a future session. I will apologize now; however, apologize again that was your experience. You are going to succeed at all you strive to do.

I genuinely believe that. You are so strong already, and I can see that you are deeply committed to this process. I see your true desire to heal and that you are willing to do the work. I am proud of you Journee. This has been a great start. I hope you are feeling ok about the process so far. If you have any questions or need to take a break we can." Dr. Stone says empathetically.

Journee nods her head, to imply she understands.

"Ok, then we will continue. We are moving along the timeline. We will discuss middle school now. So, from sixth grade to eighth grade. How were those years for you and what memories stand out the most? Dr. Stone says turning the notebook to the next section of blank pages.

Journee draws a small heart with a break in the middle of it on her journal intake page...

CHAPTER 3

"Can I go back to Elementary?"

3

Journee was feeling a bit overwhelmed. She felt comfortable with Alesha, but it does not feel good bringing all of this up. However, she is going to continue and see if it leads to her feeling better. It feels like they discussed a lifetime and that was only early childhood. Journee knows things get even more interesting in middle school...

"Ok, you may begin when you are ready. I am prepared on my end." Dr. Stone says with her pen and notebook in hand.

"Middle school. Middle school. Middle school. It's like the movie when you say *"Beetlejuice."* You have to be on the lookout! I got good at looking out, in more ways than one..." Journee lets out a small chuckle, as she puts her hand on her forehead.

"Middle school was an interesting time for me. I always enjoyed school, so most of my classes were fun. I was not the strongest in math. I am an adaptive learner if I understand the instructions. Math is not necessarily hard, but it is not explained consistently. All of my teachers were different, and how Gram talks to you; math gets your blood pressure up. Haha!

I continued singing in chorus and playing the clarinet. I loved taking sixth grade Home Economics. I learned how to make lemonade from scratch and bake chocolate chip cookies in that class. We also sewed pillows, and teddy bears from patterns. We made them by hand and using a sewing machine.

I am appreciative of that class. It deepened my love for cooking and sewing." Journee says with a slight smile on her face.

"That is great that you can acknowledge when your passion began. I love cooking as well! I learned from my adoptive mother. You are doing great. Please continue." Dr. Stone says warmly.

"I learned to cook from all the women in my family for sure. My grandma would cook quick meals during the week most families enjoyed. Spaghetti, baked chicken, and other pasta dishes. On Sundays after church, she would cook large dinners. Meatloaf, mashed potatoes, fried cabbage, cornbread, and corn was one of my favorite meals she made. If she did not cook, we would go out for dinner at *Old Country Buffet*.

Sixth grade started off smoothly. I met new people. The kids that I knew from elementary school were there, but also new kids from the four other elementary schools were there as well. It was new to see so many kinds of people. My elementary school had more white students than Black students or Hispanic students. Now it was a more balanced blend of all races.

We had a multicultural fair, and everyone had to make displays of their heritage. I did a project on being African American. I know now from my ancestry test that I am mixed with a lot more. I enjoyed the event. I invited my grandma and her friend. My grandma came dressed like me in traditional African garments, and her friend came dressed as she normally does.

She was a butch lesbian woman. She preferred to dress in male clothing over woman's clothing. As they arrived a student said..."

"Journee your grandma and grandpa are here."

"I felt so bad because she still looked like a woman despite her clothing choices. They were being rude to her, but she told me they did not know any better. I was still embarrassed and hurt by their statement. That would be the first of many examples that I would go through to learn being a lesbian was unaccepted.

"I would like to interject here. I respect the fact at such a young age you were considerate of her choices to step outside of society's norms. That was brave of both of you. We need people to be proud to be themselves in all ways, not just sexuality. We also need allies that understand a person is not a threat to them for not choosing the same as them. I ate a different breakfast than my neighbor this morning. What they ate did not affect me. What I ate did not affect them. We can be cordial when we see each other and not be involved in each other's lives past that moment. Unless we burn something, our worlds do not have to mix. Like Tabitha Brown says."

"Because That's my business, and If you can't have a good day. Don't you dare go messing someone else's up."

"I see here on your triage paperwork, that you listed your sexual orientation as Bi-sexual. I appreciate your honesty and willingness to disclose that information. We ask certain questions to help us match the best therapist for you. We Have patients request LGBTQ+ Friendly providers, male only, female only.

We have the post incarceration program as you are aware of. We also offer Sexual Trauma intensive therapy, couples therapy, family therapy, children services, and anyone going through any kind of transition in life. To join that group you may be facing a recent death of a loved one, homelessness, surviving suicide, pregnancy choices, miscarriage and pregnancy loss, infant loss, or loss of a child, postpartum and so much more. I will explain more as we go along. Can you elaborate more on how long you have known you were a Bisexual woman?" Dr. Stone asks warmly.

"Yes, I was mad at first, because I did not understand why the nurse was asking me so many questions. She was not the friendliest, so I assumed she was just being nosey.

I appreciate you explaining all of what you offer here. I have experienced quite a bit of the traumas you specialize in. I first started to notice I looked at other women how I viewed men in the sixth grade. I had my first boyfriend by the middle of sixth grade. He was popular and attractive to all the girls. I was surprised he liked me. I did not dress like the other girls at the time. I was in turtleneck sweaters and jeans that had no shape. Haha!

He told me my smile was pretty. Our relationship was "puppy love" for sure. Nothing too serious, he would hold my hand and walk me to class and the bus loop.

One day he was walking me to the bus and in front of everyone he kissed me. I mean he kissed me on my lips and held on tight. I was not prepared and became embarrassed. I broke up with him after. When I talked to my grandma's friend about it, she questioned why I did not want to be his girlfriend. I told her I did not like the kiss, and I was not ready for that yet. She asked me if I liked girls instead. I had found myself looking at the girls and feeling butterflies. I was so afraid to admit it, but of all people, I knew she would understand what I was going through. I confided in her and she gave me great advice through the years." Journee takes a moment to drink her water.

"I appreciate you elaborating on that. As we go forward in the sessions specific to that period of your life, we will dig deeper to understand where those feelings may have stemmed from. Did you have any problems with your ex-boyfriend or other boys after you broke up with him?" Dr. Stone asks calmly.

"It is funny that you ask that. Yes, actually! I had problems with him and other boys after that. I was on the bus home one day and as I was walking to my seat, I noticed a new person on the back of the bus. I normally sat at the back, but because I noticed him, I sat halfway back. I had seen him before at school, but I knew for sure he did not ride my bus. It was not long after we pulled out of the parking lot that he came to speak to me. I realized quickly that he was not on my bus by mistake.

He leaned over the seat and spoke to me. He asked how my day was. Avoiding eye contact I told him fine. He asked me to come sit with him. I told him with attitude that I was ok sitting where I was. He came to sit at the end of my seat anyway. I faced the window to show no interest in any further conversation. Talking was the furthest thing from his mind. He wanted the opposite. To shut me up. He wanted to put his penis in my mouth...

Journee says with anger and legs starting to shake again.

"I could not believe how direct he was. He never flirted with me before; he did not ask me to be his girlfriend. He simply pulled his penis out and told me to suck it. I was disgusted. I was not attracted to him. I did not want to do it. I told him no. He grabbed my hand and tried to make me touch his now erect penis. I snatched my hand back and told him to let me out of the seat. He tried to push my head down onto his penis. I pushed him away and climbed over to a different seat.

The bus driver, noticing the commotion, told us to stay in our seats. Before I could get up to tell the driver what happened, he got up and walked to the front of the bus to exit. He got off at the next stop. I watched him walk off down the street with his pants sagging off his ass. I was so angry. I wanted to fight him so badly. My stop was not long after. I got off and quickly ran into the house to shower. I felt disgusted. The bus driver did not say anything to me.

I learned years later that she called home and told them I was performing oral sex on the bus. What angers me most is that she did not say anything

63

to me before she spoke to them. If she asked me about it, I could have told her he forced himself on me. I also could not believe that she even allowed him on the bus. It was clear he was on the wrong bus, and she still let him on. I was the only person of color on my bus, and he was Black.

I was also very hurt, because my grandma did not tell me until I was grown and married. I know now they did not let me go to places or out often, because they feared what I would be doing. That hurt because I was trying to keep to myself. I did not seek him or tell him to get on my bus. I knew the way they treated me was because they thought I was "fast." I was determined not to be. The boys would not make it easy for me though, and at times, I made it hard for myself."

"Wow! I am sorry that you had to experience that. That is hurtful on so many levels. The adults failed you in that situation. The bus driver should have been more alert when allowing people to board her bus. She also did not follow any protocol for alerting someone's family about an incident that was as serious as that. She should have involved all parties and parents involved. They did not manage that well and the wrong person had to face the consequences for his actions. You. I apologize again. Please continue." Dr. Stone says visibly disturbed.

"Thank you. That means more to me than you know to hear. I love my family, and I know that they were doing their best for me. I was determined to make them proud.

Our school year had just begun. It was still warm enough to have a light jacket on. I love the fall season. That school year, America changed forever.

I was sitting in 7th grade chorus class, when the announcement to turn on the TVs came on. It was September 11th, 2001. The "Twin Towers" were on fire; and New York City to beyond New Jersey was engulfed in smoke. The attack on the world trade centers and pentagon was taking place. After seeing the news reports, the buses began rolling into the front loop. They evacuated us to go home.

When I got home my mom was there. I knew it was serious because she was crying. I sat on the floor in her room and watched the reports. Terrorism. What did it all mean? We lived in Upstate Ny, but NYC is not that far. Would the world as we know it end? This gave me worse anxiety than the Y2k scare. We spent the night in church when that happened. I thought we would be going to war and not going back to school. I did not know what it all meant. I met friends whose parents arrived home with ash and debris on them, after walking miles due to no transit running. The fear or anxiety that it put in people is felt to this day. We did not stay out of school long.

I got into a little trouble in school when we came back. I was in woodshop class. A white boy and his friend were sitting in the hallway by my locker. I was stopping to get my project coming back from the bathroom. That's when he says…"

"Nigger Monkey."

"I hoped I was tripping and asked him what he said again. He said…"

"You heard me you Nigger Monkey B. I. T. C." …

"I punched him in his face before he could say the H." Journee sighs in disappointment and clearly still disturbed by this memory.

"I broke his glasses onto his face. I thank God, he did not knock me out. He was a big man. Instead, he was more shocked, I hit him, and the teacher came soon after. So much for unity and patriotism. The school suspended me. My grandma was not happy about it. She felt I was wrong for touching him, but he should have received consequences.

I was not surprised by his level of disrespect. They were being taught to be that way. You have to be taught to love or taught to hate. Our teacher one day turned on a video, no explanation, other than it was February and black history month. She went to the back of the room and fell asleep. The video went on to explain the murder of *Emmett Till*. A young boy killed brutally for allegedly whistling at a white woman. The photo his mom released to *Jet* Magazine showed up on the screen. That image haunts me to this day. I and other students walked out of class. It was extremely insensitive." Journee takes a moment to reflect. She stares out the window quietly for a moment.

Dr. Stone allows Journee a moment to reflect on the memory. She then continues the session.

"I definitely know the story that you are referencing, and it is one of the many tragic told and untold stories of the past. I would like to commend you for feeling any form of guilt for your actions in that moment. Whilst I normally say violence is not the answer. There was no quick escape from that situation, and it was escalating quickly. You were outnumbered. I know mentally you had to have locked up, because there was no verbal response, just a physical reaction. That tells me that you reacted instantly. Your body chose to fight instead of fleeing. Fight or flight or freeze is our bodies' natural way of responding to stress or traumatic experiences.

I apologize that you had to experience such hatred. I am proud that you were remorseful and chose to rise above becoming a person like him. It is not ok for anyone to call another person, especially a stranger out of their name. For any reason but especially based on race. It is disgusting and classless behavior. Please continue." Dr. Stone says disturbed.

"I wish that I could say that it got better but it only got worse. I was doing well in my classes and always made honor roll. I enjoyed learning and really tried my hardest to do well. I started having issues with boys and not long after I was having problems with girls. I went from having friends, or at least I thought I did. However, seventh grade I was a loner. I entered my "emo phase" at this moment, and Mom I am sorry, but it definitely was not a phase. Haha!" Journee leans forward laughing.

"I laugh so hard when I see those memes online. I saw an emo emu on a poster!" Dr. Stone says laughing in agreement with Journee.

"That is too funny! Well, I learned quickly I was not a comedian. I avoid playing the dozens. I never wanted to joke with someone about something that brings them real pain. That's just evil.

So, I put my foot in my mouth one day with a girl in the lunchroom. She said she wanted to be taller. I had not seen her eat lunch often, so, no "shade" intended, I said maybe if you ate more you would grow more. Her response was..."

"Maybe if you didn't eat so much you wouldn't be so big."

"I said, well dang. I did not know I was considered to be big until that moment! I started developing and it was happening fast. I went from a tank top under clothes to a full B cup in bras in one summer. I had hips and thighs filling in my straight jeans more. I also was considered one of the taller girls at this point. I wore hand me down tees from my older cousin. He wore name brand clothes and sneakers. He was liked by a lot of people. He was like the "*Fresh Prince* Of Rochester" at the time.

I had what people considered "bobo" shoes because I wore *Sketchers*. Surprisingly, I was ok with how I dressed. Only others tried to make me feel bad about it.

Things got dramatic with the girls and my grandma came to speak with us. I was in therapy with the school guidance counselor by this point. I have dealt with anxiety, depression, dealing with suicidal thoughts, body image issues and eating disorders, and ADHD. She helped keep me on track.

She arranged for my grandma to speak with all of us girls. We were all girls of color, and she had words of wisdom for us. My grandma is a darker skinned woman. She said she has to smile, so people do not feel intimidated by her. She showed me the movie *The Imitation of Life* growing up. It helped me understand colorism, and the damaging effects it has had on generations of people. She used that as an example while speaking to us. They were polite and listened for the moment. Then, I overheard them once she left making jokes and being disrespectful. I confronted them, so they knew I heard them and slammed the door storming out. If I did not leave, I was going to get into a fight and possibly get suspended again. I was over trying to make friends. I was cool being on my own.

I dumped the cool boy, who was even cooler now. He got taller and had hair now. He ended up dating a girl I thought was a friend to me. I managed to avoid him and most drama until one day I was going to the bathroom during class. My ex was coming out of the boy's bathroom, as I was walking up to the girl's bathroom.

He barely acknowledged me most days, but he was quite friendly at that moment. He asked me how I was doing, and I told him I was ok. He tried to give me a hug, by putting his arm around my neck. He was flirting with me trying to convince me to come into the bathroom with him. I told him no thank you and rushed into the girl's bathroom, assuming he could not come in. I was wrong. He opened the door as quickly as I was closing it. He said..."

"Shit, I'll come in the girl's bathroom that's fine."

"I told him no. No. NO. I push him back into the hallway. At this point he has his arm around my neck again and pulls his penis out and says…"

"Come on suck it."

"He pushed my head in the direction of his penis. I had not had sex yet and did not want to start like this. I told him to stop and reminded him that I was not his girlfriend anymore. He still tried to push me down. I have one hand holding me up and one knee. I am ashamed to say as I was about to give up and perform oral sex on him in the hallway.

Where we were standing, anyone could come to use the restroom. There were large open windows behind me that viewed into the other hallways and lockers. I looked up and saw the security cameras. I gasped and pointed at them immediately. I said, "Look, they have been able to see us this whole time!" He quickly put his penis back in his pants and took off. I did not speak to him anymore after that.

I did not talk to any more guys for the rest of the school year.

I met a guy, and we dated the last two months of the school year. He was a transfer from another school and a grade ahead of me. He was smooth dark chocolate and had braids like Mario. I liked his smile. I was finally prepared to kiss if the moment presented itself. It did, and it was nice. He was leaving though, so we chose to break up. We made the best decision for both of us in that moment. I felt like "Corey and Topanga" from *Boy Meets World*, minus the cheating! I will never forgive Corey. Haha!" Journee says laughing.

"I loved that show! I watch *Girl Meets World* with my girls. That was such a good idea. I also agree that ending the relationship was best. Distance puts a strain on relationships that adults struggle to balance, let alone young love.

I am proud of you all for being mature about it at such a youthful age. I would like to commend you for standing on what you believe in. The best lesson I have ever learned is No is a complete sentence. No. That is all you have to say. Anything after that is rape.

It is grounds for you to defend yourself and your children, by any means necessary.

You do not have to be ashamed that you almost gave in. You liked that man at one point, and it may have been something you wanted to happen, but not in that way. Not in a public space. He did not show you value or respect at that moment. The saddest thing is that he did not have any respect for himself. I mean this with love; regardless of how he felt about you, he should have valued himself more.

I have so many male patients that have to learn self-control and self-love. How to read queues and what CONSENT means. I am so happy that I know you are happily married with children, because you deserve genuine love. Love from a man who is going to respect you and value you despite your past experiences. I am proud of you for still giving love and men a chance. Please continue." Dr. Stone says warmly.

"Thank you. The summer before eighth grade was cool in the summer. I was riding bikes and made a new friend. She moved to our neighborhood. I would go and hang with her and her family briefly. My grandma did not play about me being in anyone's house. My classmate invited me to a sleepover on the same street as us. She walked me there and came back before we got to even cut the cake!

I joined the track team. I played soccer for our local team. My mom signed me up for traveling basketball. I loved basketball, but to that point I had only played around in our backyard. My cousin, his friends, and my grandpa would play back there until the mosquitoes ran them out. I almost ruined my career early.

One night my cousin and his friends were watching scary movies in the living room. I rarely got to be with the boys, but I was quiet! They asked me to go turn the light off in the back. I was terrified, but he pushed. I ran so fast to turn the light off and back to the living room that my adrenaline kicked in. So much so that a hook from the metal hanger was stabbed into the bottom of my foot. My cousins friend noticed my slipper was wet. All I could think of was the movie *Mommie Dearest* and hearing Joan Crawford's character saying…"

"NO MORE WIRE HANGERSSSS!"

How was that my mom's favorite movie, but she has a closet full of wire hangers at the time! I also hear Madea saying it too now. Haha! My mom had to take me to get stitches! I tried out for the basketball team and did not make it in seventh grade. It crushed me, maybe the hanger incident was why!" Journee says laughing and sipping her water.

"That is hilarious and not funny at the same time Journee. I am so glad you were ok. I love those movies, especially *The Imitation of Life*. I cry every time. I am a biracial woman. I am often asked "what are you mixed with?" People assume because I am lighter skinned that I am mixed with Caucasian and African American. I am half Hindu Indian and half Catholic Puerto Rican, raised by Southern Pentecostal Caucasian Americans! I had to do my DNA as well. That was very profound of your grandma for attempting to lead the village. That is how she was raised and that way of teaching is why the world still goes to this day. Through the will of God of course! Please continue." Dr. Stone says smiling with pride.

"I kept practicing and made the team by eighth grade. I loved eighth grade. Playing on a team was good for my self-confidence. Teamwork Makes The Dreamwork is big facts when it comes to sports. The bus rides after a win were the best!

All the boys had tried and failed at this point. I was officially single and completely ok with it. I was so single I could not land a date for our eighth-grade formal. Haha! The boy that I liked by then was not into me.

I love my mom and grandma. They still dressed me up and made me feel beautiful. I had my first LBD aka "little black dress," with spaghetti straps to show just enough skin! I had cute strappy heels to match. They got my hair braided and I had small diamond studded butterfly clips on each braid. I can say that eighth grade owes me nothing! I had no idea how unready I was for high school. We took a tour of our high school. It looked so big to me at first.

I saw my older cousin and went to speak, and he completely embarrassed me in front of everyone. He treated me like a nerd and told me to get away from him. Like I did not have the right to speak to him in public. I was so sad because I always looked up to him. He later explained that it was because there was nothing but guys over there. He did not need them "all up in my face or me all up in theirs." He has a daughter of his own. I understand now and am thankful for him being respectful to me and his real friends were too. I still learned the hard way what he meant by them being all up in my face. He would graduate that year, and I would enter right after him.

"Wow, Journee. I am in awe of your strength and ability to keep smiling through adversity. You came into this session with all the jokes and smiles. I am learning now that you have overcome so much you deserve to smile. But I also want you to feel free to be vulnerable.

It is ok to be angry, you can cry, you may not have the words for how an experience makes you feel. They treated you like an object for sexual needs. They did not value you as the queen you are, or a human being for that matter. I am sorry that they did not have someone guiding them with love and wisdom to spread kindness. I never make excuses for the behavior of attackers: however, I do acknowledge every action stems from somewhere.

I have to say again that I am so glad that you have a husband and family that loves and appreciates you. I know that we are at the beginning of a long road to full recovery and healing, but I am so confident in your success and likelihood of finishing this program successfully.

We are going to take a brief break and then we can continue discussing your first year of high school." Dr. Stone gets up to exit the room.

Journee decides to change seats. She moves to a sky blue bean bag on the floor and grabs a bag of BBQ chips from the snack display...

CHAPTER 4

"9ᵗʰ grade nightmares"

4

"I did not make it past ninth grade before they decided to put me in an all-girls school. After seven years My mom had fallen in love again and my little brother would make his entrance to the world at the start of my 9th grade year. Yes, high school was even more interesting than middle school." Journee takes a deep breath.

High school is a time when you define who you will be in your next stage of life. Hormones are also raging and controlling the minds of most teenagers. Journee was no different.

"Ok, let's get back to the timeline. Tell me about ninth grade year. We will break 9th grade and your remaining three years of high school into two time periods, because you mentioned you changed schools. You can begin when you are ready." Dr. Stone says with her notebook open to a clean page titled ninth grade.

"Ninth grade feels like a bad dream when I look back. My mom was married and pregnant. I gained cool step siblings. My mom was sick throughout her pregnancy. My little brother was born prematurely. I did not want to see her or him in the hospital. It caused tension with my stepdad and me. He thought I cared more about being at my grandma's house than being there for my mom. I did not want to see her sick. Yes, I wanted to live at my grandma's house, but that was not why I did not want to be there. It was hard to see my brother with all the tubes and machines. He wanted me to live with them and that would mean I would change schools. I was already on a team. I was learning who I was. I did not want to leave. Little did I know that I would have too anyway.

I was doing well in my classes. I had one teacher complaining to my parents about my behavior in class. She called home saying I was being a disruption, and I was not. The other students would skip her class and walk out to smoke. They would come back and smell like it, and she said nothing. At most I would fall asleep. I acknowledge now that was disrespectful and only hurt my education in the long run. My mom would say the teacher has their degree already. She was right!

One day I woke up just in time to answer the question and got it right. As I was walking out the door a girl asked me to hand a boy a note for her. I handed him the note and heard my grandma's voice say."

"Oh, so we are passing notes now, are we?"

"My heart froze. My mom and grandma stood on the other side of the exit to the classroom door. I assured them I was passing the note for someone else, which I never did again. We walked in and had a conference with the teacher. My grandma wanted to know why she contacted her, and I clearly participated in class. The teacher apologized and said we would continue to work together. I passed the class but was happy to not have her as a teacher again.

I made the basketball team ninth grade year. I would catch the bus home most days, but I missed it one day. I made friends with the other players and the boys' team. I asked for a ride home from one of the boys. He would give me a ride to remember.

I did not live far from the school. Quick right and a left and I am home, but he made a left and I knew then he was not taking me straight home. He drove miles from the school and in the opposite direction from my house. We pulled up to his house. He said he forgot something and had to run in quickly. He asked me to come in. I was hesitant, but I followed him inside. We were there alone. He made his move, and we were laying on his living room floor.

I asked him if we could go to his room, and he said he did not want to risk his family catching us upstairs. But he was willing to get on top of me on the living room floor right by the door. I was officially losing my virginity. It hurt and was nowhere near as romantic as I dreamt it would be. He finished and got up off the floor. I walked around and looked at the photos on the mantel. I came to a prom photo of him and one of the prettiest girls at our school. I asked him if they were together, and he said yes. He handed me a grape blow pop and said…"

"Congratulations, you lost your virginity."

"We got back in the car, and he dropped me off. I was not his girl. We did not talk on the phone. I felt worthless. My grandma taught me early that you never want to be the girl in the room who has been with all the men there. I was trying my best to preserve any form of positive reputation I had left. I was leaving practice and another guy offered me a ride home. I told him thank you and assumed he was ok because he knew my cousin.

Based on the way he turned out of the school; I was already preparing for the bs.

Of course he drove to his house. Of course, he forgot something and wants me to come in. We got to his room, and he pulled me onto his lap. He kissed me a little and then attempted to push my head down. I stopped him and said I would have sex, but I was not performing oral sex on him. He said he did not want to have sex with me he only wanted head. I told him I did not do that. He said I could get out. I threatened to tell my family, but I left out walking.

As I was walking down the street, he pulled alongside me and told me to get in. When I made it to the main road and realized how far I was I reluctantly got in. He turned the music up and did not speak. He dropped me off at the furthest point from my house, I might as well have walked home from school.

I was home one night after that happened, and I got a call on the phone. It was him saying he was outside of the house. I told him he was tripping and hung up. He called back and told me to look out of my window. I looked out the window and saw them parked outside of my house. Literally! Directly in front of my house. I told him they had to leave before my grandma sees them. He told me he was not leaving until I came outside.

They stayed, flashed their lights, and called back. I did not want him to keep calling so I went outside. I made them pull up and met them in the curve of our street. I told them they needed to leave. That my grandma would kill them and me if she found us. He tried to make a move. They were in the car four deep. They wanted me to have sex with all of them. I told them no and told them I would call the police if they did not leave. Thankfully, they left. I know now how dumb it was to go outside. I should have just woken my grandma up."

"I can see why you would be fearful. They were outside of your home. They had breached all boundaries at that point. They were in your safe space, and you wanted them gone. I do not blame you for that. I am also proud of you for standing firm and not engaging in sexual acts you do not desire to participate in. I am so sorry that the hormones of teenage boys clouded their judgement. Not all, but when they do it is bad. Please continue." Dr. Stone says warmly.

"I got into a relationship after that. He was a football player. He was not the most popular guy, but he was not the water boy if you know what I mean. He walked me to class every day. The way he would want to walk would make me late to my classes. We would

walk connected with his arms around me. One of the teachers knew my grandma and would come down on me hard for being late. My boyfriend did not care. We walked to each class that way. One day he asked me to skip school to go to his house. I told him no. He said.."

"I know you're not a virgin, and you are my girl so what's the big deal?"

"I explained that whilst I was not a virgin, I did not want to have sex again right now, and risk getting pregnant. I did not want to be a teen mom. He did not agree, so I broke up with him.

A couple of weeks after we broke up, I was walking down the hallway. He came up to me and started picking with me. Saying little rude comments and jokingly hitting me. He then slapped me in my face. I chased him down like I was *Marion Jones*. I caught up to him as he was going out the door and I cussed him out. I told he better not ever touch me like that again. Later that night in basketball practices our coach made an announcement. We were all confused because he seemed upset. He said he was disappointed in one of us. He said he saw a display of disrespectful behavior and it was completely unacceptable. He then said he wanted a person to step forward. We all looked at each other and back at him. Looked at each other and again back at him.

He threatened that if the person did not speak up that we all would be doing nonstop suicide drills. Now as much as I like basketball. Running suicides is my least favorite drill. After moments of no one speaking up I finally put my hand up. I figured he would respect that I tried to take one for the team. Do you know this man said…"

"Thank you Journee for finally owning up to it!"

"I said, "Wait, it was really me?" He said yes and that he heard my language earlier in the day. That it was not "lady-like" nor should any of "his players" conduct themselves like that. He pushed the knife all the way into my heart. He told me he was disappointed because he thought higher of me. I tried to explain that my ex-boyfriend slapped me in the face, but he ignored me. He told me to line up for suicides and run them by myself. I felt humiliated. Infuriated would be a better word because he hit me in the face. Straight disrespected me, and I had to run laps for it.

After about six sets and feeling like I was going to throw up. My teammates one by one joined me doing the drills. They all joined me until he finally told them to stop. I was crying real tears at that point.

As mad as I was at my coach, my teammates showed me something at that moment. I felt like I let them down, but they lifted me back up. My coach did not allow me to play in our big game or dress in my uniform. It was our biggest game of the year and was in the main gym of the school. My big moment was snatched from me. Or should I say slapped from me. Basketball season ended and swimming unit began. This is where I solidified that I liked women on an intimate level.

One day after swimming class I was taking a shower to go back to class. All the girls were out of the showers by then, but two. As I was washing one of the girls came into my shower. I knew her from classes, but not to be in my shower. She surprised me by coming in. As I went to ask her what she needed, she shushed me and dropped to her knees. I asked her again what she was doing, and she said "shh!" and proceeded to spread my vagina lips with her fingers. She then began doing it with her tongue. I could not believe what was happening, but I did not stop her. It felt good. She pushed me up against the wall and continued until I orgasmed. I knew then I liked girls.

She came up and kissed me. I offered to do it to her, but she would not let me. I did not like that. I did not know what it all meant at that moment. I had turned down oral sex with all the guys, but now I was receiving it in the shower from a woman, and I did not try to stop her. I was prepared to make her my girlfriend and be a lesbian. I did not even question it. I knew I liked being girly, but I was a tomboy or more masculine than the other girls

We would go on to do that every day at the end of the swimming unit for an entire semester. We did not talk about it outside of school. One day we were on a field trip. I was sitting in the seat in front of her and another guy student. I leaned over the seat to speak to her, and she was performing oral sex on the boy. He made eye contact with me and made a face that seemed guilty and apologetic, that quickly turned to a face of pleasure. I sat down as quickly as I could before she came up to see me. I understand now why all the guys thought it was ok to ask for "head." I felt so sick to my stomach. I never told her that I saw her. I just avoided her at all costs." Journee stands up to look out the window.

"Journee. Thank you for diving deep within yourself. I can tell you are deeply committed to this process. I am amazed by the activities that you all took part in. You were so young. I am disappointed with the repeated traumatic experiences you had to go through in such a small period. I am thankful that you realized a pattern and decided to stop accepting rides home. It is sad to think you cannot simply get a ride home. I know not all men are that way, but it saddens me the fact your path crossed with so many damaged men.

I unfortunately want to draw attention to one detail you mentioned. You crossed paths with damaged women as well. The young lady did not get consent technically before touching your vagina. Whilst you may have been more receptive to the encounter, she did not get proper consent. I teach from youth to adult offender classes. Ask Then Touch! I do not want to discount that being the moment you learned that you enjoyed a woman's touch, however, I cannot ignore the errors of her ways but would not dare allow a man to slide. I am proud of you, and you have only made it to ninth grade. If you would like to wrap up anything else from this period and then we will discuss your new school and the rest of high school." Dr. Stone says calmly.

"I got into a fight, which got me suspended again. I was walking to class when an upper-class female confronted me. She claimed I was talking to her boyfriend, but I was not speaking to anyone. I tried to walk away, but she pulled my hair and knocked my books out of my hand. I blacked out and started fighting. I wanted to hurt her, and I realized in that moment the anger I was holding behind my smile. My grandma was not as mad, because I was defending myself. I hated fighting, but I am always going to defend myself.

I faded into the background for the rest of the school year. I knew I was transferring, so I tried to make it to summer break. The last memory that I have that taught me about how scandalous woman can be.

I started hanging with a girl from my gym class. She was older but had to take our class to graduate. She knew my family did not let me wear brand names, so she let me wear her all-white *Air Force Ones,* yes like the *Nelly, Murphy Lee & Ali* song. Haha! I used to want to be accepted so badly. It is sad. I let someone sweat in my shoes in gym, just to flex in her shoes for a walk around the school. Just to get clowned still.

I remember walking down the hallway and a boy made fun of me. He saw the shoes and asked right away who's shoes were they. He knew they were not mine. I ignored him and kept walking. I felt cool for the moment, and he could not ruin that for me.

I went to find my classmate who let me borrow the shoes. She was in the back hallway. She told me to come with her to get something. I did not ask where we were going, I just followed her like a dummy. She walked up to the back hallway bathroom. There was an old bathroom there. The only people who went in there smoked or had sex. I tried to stop her to see if she was aware of that, but she went in so quickly.

As I followed her in the lights were off. She locked the door. She turned them on and two dark skinned men who I knew did not go to our school stood there looking back at me. She quickly gave a one-word introduction of nicknames to me and one of the guys and disappeared into the stall with the other guy. The guy grabbed my hand and pulled me into the remaining stall. He was taller than me and had a really nice smile. His teeth were perfectly white. He was dark chocolate.

He had jeans and a crisp tall white tee. He smelled like subtle cologne and outside.

Not musty but like fresh grass. He had on all white *Air Force Ones* too. The only difference was they were probably his. I had to give mine back, although after she pulled that stunt, I should have kept them.

Anyway, he sat on the toilet and pulled me between his legs in front of him. He grabbed me like he had done it before. He touched my face gently. He told me I was pretty, and that he liked my smile. He told me not to be nervous. He could feel me shaking by this point. He was polite, but all I could think was I am going to kill her. I could hear what they were doing by this point.

He asked me did I want to do anything. I wanted to say no, but I also appreciated the way he asked. He asked with confidence, but left room for me to say no. He broke the touch barrier first, but once he noticed I was nervous he released me and asked for consent. I told him we could have sex, but I do not perform oral sex. He said OK and did not hesitate to pull out a condom. Another win in that moment. My legs were shaking from the fear of getting kicked out

94

of school. He continued to caress my arms and grab my thighs.

He grabbed my neck as he kissed me again. The fear left as the passion rose. We kissed as if we were in a committed relationship, and I did not even know his real name, or age for that matter! He did not ask for my age either. It felt like forever. My classmate and her guy were done and talking about food. We finished when he finished. He told me to stay pretty, and he would see me around. I never saw him again.

Looking back, it was for the best. I should have never agreed to engage in sex with a stranger. I did not know his STD status, or where to find him if he left a child behind. I know he had to be at least eighteen and he had car keys. My grandma would have never let me date a "guy like him" anyway." I learned my lesson and never spent time together with my classmate again. That is about it for ninth grade." Journee says, feeling ashamed of her choices.

"That was one heck of a school year. You stood on what you wanted and did not want. I do not like how the situation in the bathroom began, but I am proud of both of you for having a mature conversation.

You all established consent, used protection and enjoyed each other's company. I find nothing wrong with sexual liberation if you discuss consent and what boundaries you have from the start! But you must own every decision you make in life knowing you can't take it back or get a do over. My mother and sisters taught me to never lie on your vagina. If you consented to it then own it, but if you did not consent to it, Charge them!

Now, as for your classmate, she was not your friend; let's start there. She could have set up the homie hook up, but she went about it all wrong. She did not leave room for you to say no. That was extremely selfish of her. Another option was to leave the bathroom. You did not have to do anything. I am not judging you when I say this, but with your previous experiences I can understand you feeling obligated to have sex. Please know that then, or now you do not have to give yourself to anyone if you did not, or do not want to. Not even your husband. No means just that. No." Dr. Stone says with assertiveness.

Journee begins to tear up...

CHAPTER 5

"Too Cool for High School"

5

High school is a time when you define who you will be in the next stages of your life. You develop a lot at this time if you're paying attention. It can be difficult to adjust. Journee did her best to adjust to when she transferred to a new school.

"OK, the next section of your timeline is the rest of high school. Tell me about your time at your new school. I am ready when you are." Dr. Stone says warmly, with her pen and notebook ready.

"The summer before transferring to my new school, I spent time with family and met new people. My mom and step dad took us to *Horizon Skating Rink*. I met a guy there and eventually he became my "boyfriend." I could not meet him anywhere. I could only talk on the phone.

I arrived at my new school optimistic and excited. I was not against going to a new school. Especially one that can help me get into college.

On the first day of school, the Dean of students called me to her office. When I got to the Dean's office, she explained that they had a zero-tolerance policy for violence. Due to my record of fighting in school, she felt it necessary that I knew that information. I reminded her that I had been defending myself from bullying previously. I also assured her that I valued my education and was there for just that! I left the office thinking great. I start with a target on my back and extra eyes watching me. I was walking to find my locker and a girl called me the N word. I wanted to fight, but I remembered what the dean said.

It was not hard to make new friends. People were either friendly or acting as if you did not exist. I stood out because I was one of the few girls of color in my class. We all became associates as the years went by. I am willing to be kind to anyone who is kind to me, but I learned quickly who to speak to and who not to. I did not stray too far outside of my group.

I learned the ups and the downs of the school fast and faded into the background. I enjoyed having class with all girls. And not because I am bisexual. Girls try harder in school naturally. Being in class was healthy competition to be the smartest!" Journee pauses as she gazes over Dr. Stone's degrees and awards on the wall.

"I can agree that girls tend to outperform their male counterparts. However, I will say that the structure and conditioning of a male plays a significant role in his ability to be productive. Both genders really for that matter. If a child does not have help in the home, or having the behaviors of school reenforced at home, it makes it harder for the child to know how to ask for help. Please continue." Dr. Stone says warmly.

"I also learned how sneaky girls can be. I learned quickly how to skip class properly. I caught on to who was more financially secure, who was on drugs, who was dating. I saw everything, even if I did not say anything. I was not into drugs at this time, or at all in high school. I was team *D.A.R.E.* at the time. I was into boys though.

I finally took my boyfriend up on his offer to skip school and go to his house. I wrote my fake note and got a pass to leave class. I could not believe that it worked. I was so nervous. We had a small, abandoned bathroom at the backside of our school. It is in the old gym. I would always hide in there to use the bathroom. Having Crohn's disease sometimes I would throw up or sometimes my stomach makes a bathroom soundtrack that I am not fond of serenading others with. So, I would hide in there to use the bathroom. I was sick to say the least, but I got it together and went to stand at the exit.

He pulled into the loop to pick me up. I could not believe I was doing this. I got in and he smiled. I could see he did not believe I would leave as well. We went straight back to his house. We went to his room. His room was big enough for his bed and large tv. So, sitting on the bed was the only choice. The setup did not leave room for much foreplay. He started kissing me. He turned on, Oh my God, I cannot believe I am saying this, but of all people's music. *R. Kelly, Honey Love.* As a survivor of sexual assault, I have struggled with to listen or not to listen to his music now. I would be lying to say he is not musically a genius; however, it left me conflicted by it all.

Anyways! We started having sex. He had me get on top of him and I felt so insecure at that moment. I did not feel sexy, I felt worried that I was going to get in so much trouble. I wish I had of waited. It could have been special if we waited for the weekend together, but not skipping school. Thankfully, he got me back to school safely and not with a child. My husband always says God looks out for babies and fools. I was a foolish baby at the time. I decided not to leave school with him anymore.

We continued to talk on the phone and one night he convinced me that he would take care of me and that I could come live with him. I know it sounds so obviously crazy now. At that moment I wanted to believe he was telling the truth, and it was fate. So, I decided to jump out of my window and walk to the Mobile gas station to meet him. I made it to the gas station. He was not there at first. This was at a time I did not have a cell phone, so I had to just wait. Finally, he pulled up on the side of the building. As I was going to go out the door, my grandma pulled up on the other side. I froze, but my heart was racing. She hopped out the car with a look that I know to this day killed me! She told me to get in the car.

When we got back to the house there were police there. They called P.I.N.S. (Person in need of supervision) on me. They said if I did anything like that again I would be on watch. I swore it was the first and last time. I am grateful God heals and forgives, or I would be dead." Journee says with a dismal stare out the window.

"I applaud your grandmother for trying to get you help. She did the right thing, by getting you into a new school environment. She sacrificed for you to have a good future. I am thankful that, God protected you in that moment. Ugh! You were almost taken away by a man. He should not have been talking to you let alone picking up a teenage girl from her home. I would like to briefly address your reasoning behind agreeing to leave. What about leaving seemed better than staying home?" Dr. Stone asks warmly.

"To be honest with you. I had moments of dealing with suicide at this point in life, I felt unloved or unwanted at times. I felt like a burden and assumed they were better off without me. I know now I was so wrong. I do not know what woke her, or how she knew where to find me. I am so glad she did!" Journee says with a genuine smile.

Dr Stone smiles back warmly and says, "I am too. Please continue with the rest of your story about high school."

"Well clearly that relationship was over. Haha! I continued the rest of the school year focused on school and sports. I tried out for my new school's basketball team and did not make it. It bummed me out because I played for years at this point. I decided to apply for a job.

I worked at *McDonald's* for about a month and then I resigned. It was not at all what they promised in my interview. I thought I would be the cute cashier talking to everyone. NO. I was in the back. On the line. I had about one day of video training and a walk through. I was making burgers during rush hour. Back there burning myself on the deep fryer. I was over it and so was my mom.

I finished the school year by the skin of my teeth. Their curriculum was a bit more advanced than my old school. I ended up having to do summer school to catch up

At the end of the school year, we had a school dance. I was so excited because my mom and grandma let me go. They stayed parked outside in the parking lot, but it was a step in the right direction after such a rough start. I had a guy asked me to dance. He seemed cool. He was tall and brown-skinned. He had dimples and a shockingly bright white smile. I thought he was cute. We talked for about 5 minutes, and I asked him did he wanted something to drink. He said sure, so I told him I would be right back. I got the drinks, and by the time I got back he was tonguing down another girl.

I was absolutely disgusted, and I also felt rejected. If I could turn red, I would have been as bright red as a tomato at that point. I turned to leave, and noticed another guy had seen the entire moment. He quickly interjected and said his friend was a dummy, but he didn't mean any harm by it. He said he probably just thought I wasn't coming back. He was as tall as the friend, if not taller. He was darker skinned, but I liked that. He had a genuinely nice smile and smelled amazing. He asked me did I wanna dance with him. I said yes and we danced all night long. We were all sweaty at the end, but it was fun

I made it home in one piece, because mom and gram were in the handicap spot right in front, could not miss them. Haha!

I met a new guy at the mall. I knew of his family, so we started talking as friends for a while. He said that he was 19 years old, but I think he may have been older. I was 14 years old. He was into sneakers like I was. He asked me if I wanted to go sneaker shopping. He worked at the sneaker store and got a discount. So, I told him which ones I wanted, and I said

I would pay him to bring them to me. He insisted that I had to be with him, because he could not return the sneakers if they did not fit. So, I unfortunately skipped school again. I watched all of my friends leave on a regular. They would get food, get their nails done, and have a good time.

That was not the case for me this time. Like the other situations, we did not drive anywhere close to the mall. He drove straight to his house. He said that the sneakers were inside. I told him that I wanted to wait in the car. He said no to come inside because someone could see me. It made since because he lived close to my church.

Long story short he did not have the sneakers, but he did force me to bend over in his living room. I felt so stupid for falling for this game again. Guys think being pushy is ok, but I put myself there, so I blame myself. He dropped me back at school. After I went off on him, he called me a gold digger; even though I said I was willing to pay for the sneakers. Mind you, he's lying about sneakers, to take vagina from a 14 year old. I was dumb for going, but it is sad I have to assume rape or negative first. I tried to have faith in black men. It hurts to say in all of my experiences, I have only been assaulted by black men.

It is not that I want white men to do it and that would have made it better. It all is traumatic for anyone that has experienced being taken advantage of. I am grateful I was able to heal and continued to give people a chance. I never spent time with him again of course." Journee says slightly annoyed thinking about the memory

"I want you to know, please do not blame yourself for wanting to do something else or not doing something you would regret later. It is still a form of rape if you say no, and they continue forward. I did not mean to interrupt, but I need you to remove that guilt. Only own what choices you made. You chose to go for shoes, it was ok to choose not to have sexual relations, but please continue." Dr. Stone says firmly, but empathetic.

"Thank you for that. I deal with thinking about my past moments. Realizing after that I was too trusting or had the wrong impression of people. I had to pray hard for discernment to know who genuinely had my best interest at heart.

I was at the mall for a job interview at the pretzel place. My mom and grandma waited for me in the food court. I finished my interview, excited that I got the job. When I met up with mom and gram at the food court, I saw the boy that asked me to dance once his friend bailed on me. I asked my grandma if I could talk to him. She said yes so, I jumped right up.

He saw me coming and immediately started walking towards me. He acknowledged that he remembered me. Then he ushered me towards the door. He told me that he wanted my phone number, but I had to go across the food court to his cousin and give him my phone number. As crazy as it sounded, I went and gave his cousin my phone number. He claimed he had his phone. My grandma thought that it was strange, but I was so excited.

To my amazement he messaged me. And not long after he would become my boyfriend. Life was coming together. I had the perfect job. I was doing good in school. And I had a boyfriend who was smart, handsome, and charming. Until that charm wore off and reality set in...

I was working one day at the pretzel place and three girls walked up to speak to me. One of the girls claimed to be my boyfriend's real girlfriend. She found me online and said I stole her boyfriend. I told her that I had no idea what she was talking about. She explained they were dating, and it abruptly stopped. I apologized to her even though I genuinely had no idea what was going on, and I told her I would talk to him about it.

I called him on the phone to tell him what happened. He knew he could not lie. He explained that the day that I met him in the mall that she was inside the arcade. That is why he had to have me give my number to his cousin. He had to get me away from her. He apologized to me and promised he did not want to be with her. That they were just friends and had not done anything but kissed. So, it was true. I felt horrible

We continue to date. I eventually met his parents. That was the best part of our relationship. Not having a dad, I was able to experience that relationship through his dad. His mom is phenomenal. She is an amazing cook and taught me great recipes that I still cook to this day. They took me to see the play, *The Lion King,* and that was such a wonderful experience.

It was not long, before it was time for us to have sex. This time I was ready. We were still young, and his parents were home, so I was nervous. I knew I wanted to be with him sexually and we talked about all the options. We talked about birth control and getting tested.

We got in the bed and started kissing. He was a great kisser. The kissing led to him undressing me. He did the same. He got on top and entered me with himself. For the first time it felt right. I was with my man, and he felt good to me. His arms and abdominal muscles were so muscular, and his dark chocolate skin glistened in the light of the window. He was an athlete, so he was strong, but affectionate with me. He made me feel special and appreciated at that moment. When we finished, he started singing…"

"I lost my virginity."

"His song caught me off guard because he said he had sex before. He lied. In that moment I felt like a whore. This was the moment I wished for. My moment that was worth waiting for. I chose to be there, and I did not feel cheap or used or forced. He told me it was ok that I had, and he did not. He said we were going to make up for it. He was right.

To the point it was all we really did. We would eat and hang out with his parents for half a show and then upstairs we'd go! It got to the point where I was doing stupid stuff to keep him satisfied. I never skipped school, but I snuck out of my mom's house once. He called me and said he was with a homegirl of ours. They were coming to pick me up to hang out. I told them I could not go, because my parents were already asleep. I knew how to get out of my grandma's house, but this house was different. He said if I loved him, I would come.

She told me to stop being scared! I went like a dummy. I almost killed myself trying to get out the window it was higher than I expected. I scraped my legs and arms all up on that windowsill and brick. ha-ha! We drove to her house to hang and then she brought me back. I tried not to be insecure about her dropping him off after me. I had trust issues by this point. I made it back safely, but I never did that at their house again. When I think about it now, I get sick to my stomach. To think I could have died out there in an accident or worse and my family thought I was sleeping. I pray over my children and the world often." Journee paused as she gazed out the window.

"Ok, back to the rest of high school. My boyfriend had an accident and was in the hospital. His friends called to tell me. My grandma took me to see him. I was glad he was ok, and it was the first moment

I realized I cared for him and loved him. The thought of him not being ok, I could not breathe until we got to him.

A few days after he was still home resting. I loved this man so much, that I convinced my bus driver to drive me to his house to drop off cards and gifts that I had for him. Can you imagine a full-sized yellow school bus crammed on a small side street. People were looking, as I got off to run up and give it to him and ran back to the bus. My bus driver was my therapist/mom. She gave me such great advice, and she supported my dreams. I started selling cookies in my junior year and she trusted me to make her son's birthday cake.

Back to his ass. Ugh! Sorry! After all that I was doing to be the best girlfriend in the world. Do you know that this man still cheated on me. Like I pulled up on you in a bus in high school and you cheat. YUP! I was working that night. He came to my job with his cousin and the girl he cheated on me with. She seemed nice. They went to a party together later. He was mad, I could not go as always. That night my cousins were over. I had not heard from him since I was at work.

This night clearly was all bad. My cousin took my phone to call someone she knew to come to see her. I caught her in the driveway.

I mean BOLD. I went out the window. I told her they had to leave and went back in. Mind you to this day she swears on her life they were there for me. Girl bye I had my own man to worry about and never had an issue finding guys. I did not need to get into trouble. I had more freedom and could work. I had matured and was gaining my trust back, and she messed that up for me.

During all of this I missed his call. When I called back, he did not answer, me being hopelessly romantic; I left a message on his voicemail. I told him that I loved him, and I played *Ginuwine Differences*. Ugh to this day I hear "My whole life…" and I change the station

He was cheating while I was leaving voicemails. With the same girl he introduced me to. I was nice to her, and she sleeps with my boyfriend. Or gives him head. I heard more than one story but guess how I found out?" Journee says with sarcastic enthusiasm

"How did you find out?" Dr. Stone asks genuinely interested in the rest of the story.

"A good friend of mine called me. We are still friends to this day. I am so thankful to her because people are afraid to tell you the truth. He clearly was not going to tell me himself. She told me she overheard them all bragging about it at the restaurant. She apologized, but I told her she did the right thing. He was wrong. I appreciated her honesty

He apologized, but I wanted to break up. He told me that was not an option. He put a poem on *Myspace*, something about his "brown skinned angel...blah blah blah," boy bye! Where was this before breaking my heart and embarrassing me? I ignored him for quite a while. He had his friends bring me teddy bears. The same friend who dipped on me for the girl at the dance. I honestly was over being in their friend group. I did not trust anyone.

We stayed together until I went to college. I was doing well in school. I joined the *D.E.C.A. (Distributive Education Clubs of America)* team for school and was competing on a state level with them. I advanced to the round out of state, but grandma was not having that. They did let me do the event in

Rochester and we got to stay at the *Hyatt* downtown. I met people I would be going to college with. We won the competition as well. It was a lot of fun!

I was sitting in class one day and the girl behind me pulled my arm back when I went to raise my hand. She joked I raised it too much, but she hurt me. I was in a sling a week later in lunch. I suddenly felt a grape hit me on the head. A green grape! I looked around and saw the girls at the end of the table laughing quietly. So, I lobbed it back with my left hand. I thought that was the end of it.

Nope! I hear my name called to come to the office. Her mother wanted to press charges on me for assault. They claimed the grape scratched her eye cornea. I could not believe they were serious. I explained they threw it first and I thought it was a joke. This same girl was driving with me one day. I was not supposed to have anyone in the car, but wanting to be cool and hardheaded, we went to get food. I got into a small fender bender of course! God always had a way of showing me the error of my bad decisions quickly! But I say all of that to say I thought we were friends playing around. I explained that I am in a sling from a student forcefully pulling my arm, but I did not say she assaulted me.

Thank God, they did not expel me from school. They gave me in- school suspension. That was actually a funny experience! They left me in a small unused classroom alone for the day. By the end of the day the principal came in livid. She threw down some papers and asked me did I make them. I read the papers. They were all different variations of funny sayings. "Like happy birthday free Journee." As hilarious as it was, I had nothing to do with it. She stormed out of the room.

I loved my job. We had so much fun in that little pretzel shop. One day Beanie Man came to the mall, because he was in town for a show. My Manager had me jump the counter and run to get his autograph. I do it and as I am approaching them his security said,

"She comin' man, she coming!"

"Beanie Man laughed and signed my napkin. I was doing well in school, but I was over my relationship. It must have read in my energy, because one night I was cleaning up the store and a guy approached me.

He was light skinned and very friendly. He kept making jokes to make me laugh. I told him I had a man. Even though I technically tried to break up with him.

116

He asked what that had to do with him! I said well excuse me. He was definitely giving "bad boy vibes," but he had sex appeal. He flirted me right out of my phone number. I know now that was wrong. Do not change who you are because of someone else's actions. If you do not believe in cheating and get cheated on, don't cheat, Leave!

One night we were talking on the phone. I was talking big about what I was going to do to him. He said he was going to pull up on me. I said yes, ok, but he was serious. He came to my grandma's house. He asked to come out and when I declined, he said he was coming in. This was all my fault. I should never have told him I wanted to see him. He stood on business, and the snow in front of my window.

He came in through the window and my heart was racing. At this point in life, I did not have a doorknob on my door. That was my punishment I used a sock to be able to lock it. So, not only could my grandma or her friend come right in, but they could stand and look in first before they open the door. I told him he had to leave before.

He told me he did not come all that way for nothing. I knew where he was going with it, so I kissed him and ushered him back towards the window. He kept kissing me and grabbing my shorts. We were going to have sex whether I wanted to or not. So, I pulled my panties down and bent over. He got on the floor behind me and entered me. He was huge. The light from the tv lit the room up. I stared at the hole in my door prepared to die if she caught us.

He finished and I quickly got him out of the house. I told him I could never do that again. I skipped school with him once. I knew how to do that and felt it was the lesser of two evils. That time was actually desired and romantic. We were at his house alone. I realized that he was over eighteen. I was 15 years old and turning sixteen. We talked and joke for a while and then went to his room.

I realized in this moment the difference of being with a man more experienced than you. We were able to be completely naked. That was the first time for me. He got on top of me and kissed me. I prepared for him to enter me, but he began kissing down my body and eventually began kissing my vagina. I had been having sex, but my boyfriend did not do that to me yet. He continued. I felt things I had never felt before.

We cooked waffles after. I wanted to be with him and only him, but I was learning quickly that his life and my life were not compatible. I never snuck out of school again after that.

I did not stay at the pretzel place. I got a job at the fashion store next door. I did not work there long. Of all people the older sister of the girl he cheated on me with worked there. They also refused to let me leave for a funeral. I stated it was my cousin. I guess one of my coworkers knew of him and said we were not blood. Mind you, the night he passed on his motorcycle, he was just at my grandma's house with my cousin. He was family.

The last straw was the night before SATs my manager held me late, being spiteful. She had me folding clothes despite my grandma coming to the gate several times. The last time she told me to come on out and that I quit. That was that. Hah!

I ended up getting a new job at *Foot Locker*. That was one of the best companies that I have ever worked for. I loved my job. I worked for them off and on from 2006 to 2014. That time period in music, sports, and entertainment was exciting. I enjoyed selling shoes. I did not like Jordan release days though. Haha!

I also did not like a certain manager that worked for the other store. All of our affiliate stores come and drop money at our store. I saw this manager often, but he did not technically work at our store. One night he had to cover for my management to go for a conference. His wife and kids had come to visit. As we were closing down the store, he came into the back by the bathrooms as I was leaving out. He made a slick remark, and I let him know I had a man and remined him that his wife and kids just left.

He did not care. He came in the bathroom anyway. He pushed me over the sink and forced himself into me. He continued thrusting until he heard our coworker say the other managers were at the gate. He quickly stopped and went out on the floor. He did not wash his hands or say anything to me.

I gathered myself the best I could and went back out to finish cleaning up the store. I could see the look of suspicion on the other store managers' face. He asked if everything was ok. I was terrified, so of course I told him that I was fine. It is not like I could say, Oh by the way I have blood in my Underwear from ol' boy raping me, and that I felt ripped open. Or how I was crashing out in my mind about how to tell my boyfriend about it. He gave me a look that he knew I was not telling the truth." Journee pauses and tears start filling her eyes.

"Journee look at me. You did not cheat. You do not have to hold that guilt. He raped you. Your boss. He was someone who was supposed to be your superior. That should never have happened. You were underage. It was all wrong. I am so sorry that happened to you. We will go deeper in a later session of course, but I need you to start forgiving yourself now. Let all of that go please! You may continue when you're ready." Dr. Stone says slightly choked up.

"Well, he was not the first, and unfortunately far from the last to take advantage of me sexually. Remember the cousin from the south. He made his move on me twice since being kids. The second time he performed oral sex on me as a teen upstairs while our family was downstairs. I am ashamed to say that time I wanted it just as much as he did. The last time I was dating my boyfriend and told him no. We were there for a funeral and were supposed to be going to grab something and come right back. He pulled off a side road and forced me to have sex in his car. After that he messaged me and said he wanted us to be together. He learned we could move to California and be together legally. I told him no and to leave me alone.

Thankfully for life he did. I never told my boyfriend what he did.

I always wondered if he knew. They say guys can feel the difference in us, but I was not sure. The way he treated me, maybe. One day we had off from school, so my boyfriend had the house to himself. He wanted me to come over, so we could have sex all day. I was with it, but my Grandma was on it. She said I was not about to be in them people's house and they are not home. I had gifts for him like always, so I begged for hours until she agreed to bring me to drop the gifts and that is it. I had 5 mins she said, not even.

I went inside and he was standing in the doorway with his robe on. He said let's go upstairs. I told him that my grandma has the car running and I can only drop the gifts off. He got mad and said she was being extra. I told him maybe so, but I had to go. He said no and started kissing me. He told me to lay down on the floor. I could hear her honking the horn at this point. He was already naked and ready. He pulled my shorts to the side and entered me. He thrust inside of me. I kept saying stop, she's going to come up to the door. I don't think he even locked it. She was honking and he was humping. I could not believe the same walkway, that I once felt so happy to arrive on, would always remind me of him showing me exactly what I meant to him. NOTHING! He did not respect me or my grandma. It makes so much sense now, that is why he never came to my house. He knew we could not do anything.

He would continue to show me no respect. He stood me up two years in a row for prom. He could have said no that he didn't want to go. Instead, he got me excited, just to leave me hanging. Junior year we had an entire party at my house. Everyone else had their dates. They arrived on time and took pictures. I was alone because he had a game. Other players were on time, but I had to pay extra to have the limo pick him up at his house.

Senior year we received an invitation from our classmates to a grand pre prom event downtown. We were there for cocktail hour and appetizer plates. All of our parents were there and family members. It was a gorgeous venue. Everyone was taking pictures on this beautiful estate and once again I was alone

By this point in life, I had made friends with some lesbian women. I became very close to one of them. She and I had spent time together a few times and she was cool. She knew my boyfriend had stood me up the year prior, so she dressed prepared to be my escort to the prom. When my mom saw her, she freaked out. She told me to tell her to leave immediately. I was so embarrassed. I appreciated that she had gone out of her way for me as a friend, but my mom was not having it. So, she left. We got in the limo and arrived at prom. I participated as much as I could and after eating, dancing, and taking pictures, I sat at a table in the corner. He finally showed up. My favorite math teacher caught one photo of us together.

I wish I had gone with my homegirl. She showed me the respect of being on time and valued my feelings. He did not. He could care less about me. I should have left him once again, but I carried him into my first year of college." Journee says with her hand to her forehead.

"Wow. Wow. Wow. Journee, you are a strong woman. You had to be strong very early. You carry it well. Do not let your moments of weakness in life define you, because the things that you have overcome would have broken the average person. You are a phenomenal woman. Don't ever forget that! Ok, you said it in your last statement. Let's talk about the college years…" Dr. Stone says turning to a new page in the notebook.

Journee draws 2007 and a girl with a cap and gown on her triage sheet of the notebook and steps out to use the restroom…

CHAPTER 6

"College was a blur..."

6

The first year of college is a time to learn, grow, and prepare for the next phase of life. Journee is about to reveal a lot about this time of her life; and being on her own.

"Ok, welcome back. I hope the restrooms were clean! Moving along the timeline, we will now discuss your young adult/ college years. I read that you dropped out of school but returned to college later. Also, you said that you met your husband there. But you were making fun of me. We have a lot more in common than you think! We will discuss that time period next. You may begin when you are ready." Dr. Stone says eagerly, with her pen and notebook in hand.

"Yes, they were very clean and well stocked. Thank you. Ok, this is where things get hectic. A lot happened in a small-time frame. I am thankful to be here today.

I was accepted to almost all of the colleges I applied to. I applied to the university that my boyfriend was going to and got accepted, but my parents told me no. They said I could not move out of state. I was so mad. I felt like we were going to get to be on our own and it would have helped our relationship. I also always loved the south. They were firm on their decision, so I committed to *St. John Fisher College.* A beautiful private college not too far from home.

I chose to major in Psychology. I wanted to become a therapist and help people manage their mental health. I received a scholarship. It included a pre semester program; where I had to stay on campus the month before school started.

This caused problems in my relationship. He felt we should be spending our last days together before he left for school. That was extremely selfish to make me feel guilty about something that was mandatory for my education. He made it all about him of course.

We were only allowed to have visitors one day out of the week. We had lights out, a strict course load, and a schedule to stick to. It was a fully immersive experience to prepare you for what college was going to be like. I can remember our program leader telling us…"

"Look to your left. Now look to your right. The person sitting there now may not be sitting there at graduation. Don't be that person."

"I was determined from day one not to be that person. I had a roommate. She was from the Bronx. She was cool. She took school very seriously. She was the perfect roommate. Our room was clean, she was smart, and a good person. I never shared a room with anyone, but family, so I was grateful. Our relationship took some damage though. I allowed my boyfriend to push me, which in the end made her uncomfortable.

My mom and grandma would visit me and then leave, so he and I could see each other for a little while. The rule was that no doors could be closed. She did not have any male guests, and preferred we not, but she understood that I had a boyfriend.

However, he was still trying to have sex. She left the room, and he laid behind me on the bunk bed. The door is technically open, but he just stroked me slowly. I felt disgusted with myself. It was disrespectful to my roommate, and I knew that. I understood and had no problem following the rules. I should have put my education first and stood on telling him no. It was only three weeks, but he acted like he could not wait. I wanted it just as much, but I had dreams and goals too. He did not let me interfere with his. Everyone thought our relationship was goals, but I cannot tell you much about our relationship other than sex.

I made friends with some of his friends. I am grateful for those relationships and memories. I enjoyed the rest of the summer program. I did well in my classes and completed the program. Unfortunately, our program leader was correct. We lost a student over the summer.

I finished the summer with my boyfriend and his friends. We went to the amusement parks. We went to the beach and had a blast. Swimming in the dark, sex on the beach and not the drink of course. We went walking on the pier, while eating *Abbot's Ice Cream*. Then it was time to say goodbye. He left for school, and I prepared to head to live on campus. My mom, grandma, little sister, and aunt all helped me get ready. I packed everything into the car, and they filled the other one.

We left out in different directions on the way to the school. I was driving to school. As I was at the corner of Chili Ave and Thurston Ave, I was remembering going into the tattoo shop on the corner. I snuck in there with my homegirl and got my belly button pierced there. I sat laughing and reminiscing about being young and dumb. I went to pull off and almost got hit head on. There was a high-speed police chase. The car almost hit me head on turning onto Thurston and as I went to go the police almost slammed into me as well. My mini fridge hit the dashboard. I had a full-on panic attack. I called my family crying. They yelled at me, and said I was being extra. They laughed that I was fine because I technically did not crash. Mind you, I was only over there because I was afraid to get on the highway at the time. I have always had anxiety driving.

I arrived at the campus eventually. I met my new roommates.

They were not as welcoming as my summer roommate, and it was three to a room. I was grateful that the dorm next to me had two girls I went to high school with, and another cool girl they got roomed with. I spent more time in their room than my own. I had almost every class with their roommate, so I would walk with her to campus a lot. She was petite, but spunky. Our dorm was across the street from the campus, so we would walk and talk.

I had other friends from my high school who went to my school. I had one of my boyfriend's friends from his school adopt me as his honorary Sis. I was excited to get involved in school. I felt so mature being on my own. I joined the dance team with my roommate from the summer program. I also got a work study job on campus. I was the receptionist of an office. I loved the job, but I was quickly seeing the difference of being on my own verses my grandma waking me up. I still worked at *Foot Locker* as well.

I Had another unfortunate run in with a guy on campus. I had a few actually. The first time was not as bad as the others. I went to the dorm of the guy I met at the *D.E.C.A.* convention. He and his roommates were supposed to be having a movie night. I got there and it was just him and I and his roommate and his girl. He told me to get on his bed to sit, because his roommate was laying in his bed with his girl on the bottom bunk.

I said no I was ok sitting in the chair. He insisted on me getting out of their way. I sat at the foot of the bunk near the stairs. He tried to get me to lay back, so I got up to leave. He knew I had a boyfriend. I climbed down and went straight out the room, no explanation. He chased me down the stairs and towards the exit yelling after me. Security noticed and came out to ask if everything was ok. I said yes, but he insisted on riding me over to my dorm. The guy went back upstairs, and I knew then to stay clear of him." Journee pauses and takes a deep breath.

"I want to commend you on leaving. You assessed the situation. Decided it was not something you wanted, and you got out of there. I am so proud of you. That took strength to say no and leave. Also, you were not wrong to be upset by your near miss experience. They could have expressed that it's a blessing that you are ok and tell you to be safe. Not everyone manages stress or confrontation well. I am glad you were ok. Please continue." Dr. Stone says writing in her notebook.

"The semester went on and I was ok for a few weeks. I would talk to my boyfriend on the phone. I did not have much going on and feared he would lose interest in me. My life was "basic." I know now I was blessed. Being young and dumb, I made up a story one day. I told him that I got into an argument with a girl just to have something to talk about.

He got annoyed and asked me if I ever have a good day. That he wished to call his girl, and she is doing good for once. I felt stupid. I did not know how to keep him interested and a new girl was showing up in his pictures and friend circle.

By this point I had taken interest in the pharmacy program and landed a job at *CVS*. I made friends who would make sure I got to and from school and work. My boyfriend's friend became like a brother to me. I was hanging with him, his roommate, and his girl more than anyone. He let me use his room because he would leave campus for a few days. I'd hang and nap in there during the day between classes, so I didn't have to walk in the cold back and forth across the campus.

One night we were all chilling in bros room. I had to meet an upper classman at his dorm for a project for our religion class. His roommate was there when I got there, but he left quickly after. You probably know where this is going. I told him I had a boyfriend. He said he had a girlfriend back home as well. He was not from New York. He pushed me back and got on top of me. He struggled to stay inside of me. I couldn't even make eye contact with him. I felt like I was in a scene from the movie *The Color Purple*. I felt like Celie with M.I.S.T.E.R. on top of her. After he finished, I got up to leave. He asked about the project. I told him that I would finish it alone.

When I got back to bros room, I went straight to his shower. I broke down on the floor in the shower fully clothed. My home girl came in and found me. She yelled for bro to come help.

They got me up, asked me what happened, and cleaned me up. My bros roommate suggested we smoke some weed. I never smoked to that point, but he said with what I had been through I needed it. He was right. We walked off campus and smoked under a giant weeping willow tree. The irony, but I was no longer weeping. I was laughing and hungry. We all went to grab late night food. They took me that week to get tested for STDs and make sure I was not pregnant. I appreciated them more than they knew.

A few weeks later I get a call from my bro to come to campus asap. I got over there as fast as I could. All the guys were piled into the laundry room looking into the lounge. I went to leave, because I was immediately against being in a group of dudes, but bro insisted I look in. I did. I wish I had not. I saw my home girl on her knees performing oral sex on the boy I knew from high school and had the movie night incident with. I was shocked and embarrassed for her. I left and never brought it up again.

I still was talking to my side boyfriend occasionally. He had a baby, and I realized I was not as special to him as I thought. He came to visit me a few times on campus.

We told people he was my brother, so my boyfriend would not get word. We are both light-skinned, so no one questioned it. He came to see me one night, and I was in my campus bros room. We ended up having sex in bros bed. He said in my ear that he was going to get me pregnant. He proceeded to finish inside of me. I was not ready for a child. I did not think it would really happen, but it did.

I found out a few weeks later that I was pregnant. Everything was going to change. I could not be with my high school boyfriend anymore. I would have to stay away from all guys. I was ok with that. I unfortunately had a miscarriage almost as quickly as I found out I was pregnant. I had one in high school from my boyfriend, so I knew the signs and got to the campus medical center right away. I was early in pregnancy, so I did not have to have any removal procedures those times. I don't think my side man believed me. He said I got rid of the baby. That really hurt me, because I was not ready, but I would not have gotten an abortion. I have taken people, but at the time I did not agree with abortions.

I was crying to my bro about it a few weeks after. He was good at giving advice, but that night he wanted to console me in a different way. He kissed me and made his move. I was completely thrown off guard.

We just left hanging with his girl. I had a huge respect for her. I told him no, that we couldn't. He progressed forward. He performed oral sex on me and then we had sex. I noticed immediately that he is wider than most men and it hurt. The moment was over, and I felt horrible. I was never going to bring it up or let it happen again.

Not long after I got a call from his girl. She found texts in his phone. He had been trying to meet up again, but I declined. She saw those. I admitted to what happened. He was in the background yelling I was a liar. I did not know I was not supposed to tell the truth. She asked did he perform oral sex on me. I told her the truth. She started spazzing out. Threatening to kill me, calling me a whore. Saying she better not see me. I prayed I would not. I did not blame her for being upset.

I was sitting in my dorm a few days later when a hard knock came to my door. It was Bro. He pushed his way into the room. I told him to leave immediately. He told me to shut up. I could smell the alcohol on him. His eyes were black and lifeless. I told him to get out and pushed him. He pushed me over the desk chair and started pulling my pants down. I tried to fight him and yelled out my boyfriend will be there tomorrow. I said he is going to know you have been inside me. He told me to shut up and proceeded to rape me bent over the chair. No gentle, no lubrication. Raw, and rough. He finished, pulled his pants up, he did not say one word. He just walked out, leaving my dorm door open.

My boyfriend made it back for thanksgiving break. He came to my dorm and of course, wanted to have sex. It would be our first time as grown people, and on our own. I missed him, but I was so nervous.

He said it immediately. As soon as he slid inside of me, he said that he thought it would have been tighter. I acted as if I did not know what he was talking about. I wanted to cry. I was so scared to tell him everything that had been going on. So, I didn't...

He invited his friends over. They were supposed to be sitting in the chairs, but they end up having sex on my roommates bed. I was so angry. They never respect me, or my space. We ended break and he went back to school. I continued with classes and was trying my best to stay to myself at this point. I wanted to go to class, work, and sleep. I was barely eating at this point." Journee pauses and takes a drink of water.

"Journee, you speak about your experiences so casually, because there were so many of them. I need you to know that no matter how many times it happened, or how it happened, it was wrong. You did not deserve that. I am so sorry that the people around you did not protect you. Your Journey, Journee, flowed fluidly along the river of trauma. At some point you had to ground on dry land. I am happy you did. Please continue, I just need you to know that you deserved better." Dr. Stone says with tears in her eyes.

"I appreciate you. I definitely became numb by this point. I did not desire sex at all. I did not want a man or a woman. I just wanted to graduate. Go figure, I did not get to do that, but I did get raped again. Drugged and raped this time.

I was sitting in my dorm one night. I was on my laptop on social media. I'd just hung up the phone with my grandma. She said the weather man was calling for a "winter blizzard," and I better not leave off campus. I assured her I was in my dorm with no plans because I genuinely was. But then, I received a message from an online friend of mine. We had not met in person. He played basketball at another school about an hour away. My home girl from high school went to his school and confirmed for me he was cool. He invited me to their school for a party. He said if they won the game we had to come.

As I was writing back to tell him thank you, but no thank you, I get a knock on the door. It was a girl I met on campus and had hung out with a few times. She saw the message and started freaking out. She asked me how I knew him, and I told her social media. She took me down to her room and to my surprise the dorm was covered in his universities memorabilia and posters. She said that we had to go to the party. I told her what my grandma said about the storm and told her no. I said that I had nothing to wear or a car. She told me I could borrow her clothes, and she would drive.

I reached out to my home girl from high school to have a friend with me, but she said it didn't sound like a good idea, and she was going to sit it out. I should have listened by that point, but "wet paint child" I just had to go. She let me borrow a black dress and her *UGG* boots. Me, her, and her friend got into her car and headed to the party. I called my boyfriend to tell him. He did not like it and got off the phone with me. I had never been to that city before. It was beautifully lit up at night. I then realized we were going to a stranger and asked the girls what if the profile was fake. She reminded me that the address was on campus. It had to be real.

It was real and so was he. You could see him as soon as you turned into their section, because he was so tall. They lived in townhomes on campus. I thought that was cool. Our dorms looked like college, but theirs looked like real apartment communities. We went inside and there was a lot more people inside than I expected. There was a kitchen to the right that had a big bowl of alcohol punch aka "Jungle Juice." I did not get a drink right away. The friend of hers that came with us had a drink.

I danced with him and his girlfriend all night. She was really pretty and down-to-earth. We all danced to *Lil Wayne's* song *Brand New*. I grabbed one cup of the punch and felt okay. I needed a bathroom break. I could not find the girls I came with, so I asked the guy who invited us to hold my drink. Looking back, I do not know why I did not take it with me...

I went to the bathroom to change my tampon. I was on my cycle. When I came back, he handed me my drink back and said..."

"It's a good thing you knew not to leave your drink lying around."

"I told him that is what my grandma taught me. That was the last memory of that moment I have until the next memory that I can remember... I woke up on my back, in a dark room. I was laying on a bed with my head laying to the left. I was not alone. I heard a voice say..."

"Yo, Yo, Yo, She's waking up!

"At that moment, I started to feel my body moving on its own. My head was throbbing and felt like it weighed a ton. I lifted my head as best as I could to center myself. I then realize that the guy who invited us was on top of me. Raping me. He was enjoying himself until he looked down and we made eye contact. He quickly gasped and pulled himself out of me. He had on a condom. I can remember that. That was a red flag for me because I am allergic to latex condoms. I also knew that I was on my period and had a tampon in. He stumbled to pull his pants up and went out the room.

At that moment, the voice of the other man in the room now had hands. He began grabbing at my body and touching my tattoo. I had just gotten one on my thigh/upper vagina area. I could hear the girl I came with knocking on the door. He quickly left. She came in the room and started asking where my clothes were. She did not realize they pulled my dress up. She pulled the dress down and told me to get up. I could not stand right away. I also could not find my phone or underwear. I blacked out again.

I came to and he was carrying me down the steps. He said I was ok, and he was going to get me to the car. He got to the front door and dropped me out of his arms. I rolled down the hill and hit the trash bin at the bottom. He came laughing and running after me. The ice from the snow was cutting my bare legs. My grandma was right. It was a full snowstorm at this point. He picked me up and put me in the back of her car. I kept saying I did not have my phone, but she pulled out anyway. I blacked out again.

When I woke up in the backseat and immediately felt the urge to throw up. I grab a bag and start throwing up blue liquid. The girl I came with told me to get out the car and throw up on the grass, because we did not know how long we were going to be there. I was confused, but she explained that the car

140

broke down. We were stranded on the highway in traffic with flashers on, in the middle of a snowstorm. I got out and ran across the thruway. I continued to be sick on the side of the highway.

I got back in the car just in time. The police arrived to take us to the *Wegmans*. That was God intervening, but I had not processed what had occurred yet. I was more afraid of getting in trouble for being underage and drinking. I did not register being raped. The officer drove us to the store, where we waited on her mom to arrive. She drove us back to campus. They dropped me off in front of my dorm and pulled out. They did not make sure I made it inside, and I still had no phone. A friend of mine found me trying to open "my door," but I had wandered to the floor below. He said he guided me to my room and closed me inside. He was a cool person. I am grateful to him. We were born on the same day.

I woke up to someone banging on my door. I know now it was a day, almost two later. It was my home girl. She said she had been calling me, but my phone was going straight to voicemail. She wanted to know how the trip was. I told her not good. She then noticed my appearance and room condition. I had vomited and urinated on myself. I told her I think something bad happened, and that I cannot find my tampon.

We went to talk to the girls I went with. They acted as if I was tripping and called his girlfriend for me.

She told me that she had my phone and underwear. That she would ship it to me. She really did. I appreciated her helping me at all.

Despite the girls I went with making it like I was making it all up in my head, or worse, that I wanted it and had casual sex with him. They said I did not want to have to tell my boyfriend I cheated, so I said I was raped.

I was in shock and could not believe their reaction to it all. I went to the hospital. My home girl went with me. She apologized for not being with me. I apologized for going. They did a rape kit on me. Took pictures of my vagina and body. Took bloodwork and gave me medicines to help prevent the transmission of STDs. It made me really sick. I have always had nervous laughter, so I was being questioned on my sincerity because I was not crying hysterically at this point. I was numb.

They finished and took my home girl back to school. They would not let her come with me to the station to give my statement. I thought that was very strange. We arrived at the station very late at night. It appeared to be closed, but there was a male detective and a female officer inside. He proceeded to ask me questions and tape record my statement. I noticed it when I walked in, but once he started playing with it I had to say something. The detective was playing with a mascot from the school, where the guy who raped me played basketball for. He continued to play with it. I asked him to stop. He turned off the tape recording and leaned forward. He said…"

"Are you sure that you didn't just cheat on your boyfriend and you're looking for an excuse out?"

"He sat back and smiled. I felt sick immediately. I asked to go to the bathroom. The female officer escorted me. As I was shutting the door she kicked it back open. Shocked and startled I went to shut it again hoping it was a mistake. She did it again. I knew then I was in danger, and they were not going to help me. I told her I wanted to go back to my dorm. They informed me that meant I was dropping the charges, and I cannot speak about it again. I said what choice do I have and let them drop me off to school.

A few days later I was in my dorm. I had a shower in the communal bathroom and came back to get dressed in my room. No one was there. I got a call on my phone saying I looked nice in my pink shirt. I dropped to the floor. The voice went on to say they knew where I was and if I did not drop the charges that they would hurt my family. They said my grandmas address. I was infuriated. I let them know I already dropped them and called the police and campus security. They traced the call but said nothing could be done.

They moved me to a single inside dorm that could not be viewed from outside.

I spoke to the friend of the girl I went with recently. At the time both of them gave the same statement saying that I agreed to have sex and that's what we went there for. I asked her did she genuinely believe that or was she forced to say so. She got kind of nasty at first, but then she acknowledged that I did state we could be going to a stranger. I called my boyfriend and told him we were going, and they saw us argue. I started to regret going.

She acknowledged that. I gave her my recollections of events. She expressed that she apologized that was my experience, however, what was the point of bringing it up now after all of these years. I let her know that I just needed to know that the two WOMEN that I went with did not set me up. Regardless of what happens to him because God will have the final judgement. I wanted to know that you all did not condone rape. She said of course not, and we ended there.

But, back to how my boyfriend responded to it all. He decided to break up with me because I got raped. Of all times I was dealing with a breast cancer scare. They found a lump and removed it to have it biopsied. I was showing him where it was, and he told me to put my shirt back on. Then he broke up with me. He said it was too much for him. Like seriously, too much for him.

Then, do you know as this jerk is dropping me off, after dumping me, he proceeds to come in for a kiss. He puts his hands in my pants. I pull back, but he pulls me in.

He fingered me and kissed me passionately. For the last time. I knew it was the last time because I asked him why would he do that and what did it mean? I asked did he want to stay together. He said no and that he just wanted to say goodbye. He unlocked the door for me to get out. He was just nasty. All of the things I loved about him were no longer visible. I was so angry. I felt so used and discarded. It was ok though because I wanted to be done with him anyway. There was no love there, just lust.

I was right about the girl in the pictures too. She called my phone to let me know he was hers now. I told her I did not care. She told me that I did. I laughed and hung up. I knew what she was getting, and she would learn. I guess she thought she was one of the "*Mean Girls*," like the *Lindsay Lohan* movie. They did not stay together long.

Like a dummy I met up with him one last time. It was his birthday, and I heard he was in town. I got his favorite kind of cake and went to see him. He had me pull up with the gifts, just to ask me did I want him still. He asked if I wanted to see what his "grown man dick" was like. I still had feelings for him at the time. I knew I was not perfect to him in our relationship either, so I was willing to give it a chance.

I said yes, and then he said he was good and that he was not attracted to me anymore. I once again allowed him to humiliate me. The thought of being his queen and him my king had long faded. That was the last time I allowed him to disrespect me. I started the next semester in my new dorm and was determined to keep going." Journee says with pride.

"Journee, I am so sorry that you had to go through that. I am disgusted by all of their actions. I am proud of you for fighting to keep going. I imagine that had to be hard for you continuing on in school and seeing those girls. I commend you for asking the girl you went with those questions. I pray that brought you the closure that you deserve." Dr. Stone says disturbed, but grateful.

CHAPTER 7

"No Place like a home…"

7

At this point life was real and moving really fast. Journee was grateful to be alive. She was also grateful to have a home. Many times, she was homeless, and living with others…

"Yes I have a better peace these days with all of my experiences in life. School got pretty interesting after all of that happened. I was newly single for the first time in 4 years. Everyone I went to high school with messaged me to question why my profile said single. I felt worthless at this point. I lost my identity. I was going to therapy at the *Planned Parenthood* downtown. I am so grateful for those women during that time.

I had a few friends during this time. I was single and planned to stay that way. My side boyfriend was still coming to visit and would take me to get groceries. I was starting to catch feelings for him on a deeper level, but his lifestyle did not leave room for me. One night he came to take us out. He took me and my two home girls out on the town. At the end of the night, he lets me know he is moving. I realized he was saying goodbye. My home girls were being haters and would not go back to their dorm. So, he and I had to say goodbye in the lounge.

I was realizing more and more they were not my friends.

I was coming back from work one day and there was a party on campus. I showed up in my lab coat straight from work. I went to speak to my home girl who was clearly drunk already. I told her to come with me to get dressed and we will be right back. I could see that she had her hand down some guys pants. She was introducing him and just met him. I told her to come on and she took her hand off of him and slapped me in the face. I turned and walked away. If I stayed I was going to risk getting kicked out.

I went back to my dorm and went to sleep. I got a call on my phone saying that I had to come and help her. I told them she would be ok, but they said it was serious. This would be the second time I had to help a friend who drank too much back to their room. I had my friends help me pick her up and get her back to the dorm. We had to avoid security, and she could have cost all of us our education. After it was all over I went to meet her in the lunchroom. She was sitting with a group of upper classmen. Apparently she told them I was not a good friend and left her. I looked her dead in her face and said I will speak to you over there. I am not going to address this in front of everyone. Despite her trying to throw me under the bus I still tried to respect her.

I was talking to one guy as a friend, but he ghosted me after I broke up with my boyfriend and the rape happened. He said he did not want me to try and jump into a relationship with him. That he was not ready. Crazy thing is I didn't ask. I liked one guy, and it seemed like he liked me.

We went out and had a great time. I invited him back to my room. He was a complete gentleman. I was prepared to have sex. We started kissing. He began to perform oral sex on me. When he finished, I thought we were going to have sex, but he said he wanted to wait. I was shocked. Most guys don't do just that. He left and told me to call him later.

I woke up the next day to get food. As I was coming out of my dorm, he was coming out of the dorm of the girl across the hall from my dorm. She was friends with my home girl, but she was not fond of me. I was not fond of her either. She smiled as if she had won a prize, but he was just with me. I was sickened and never called him back.

There was a lot of sharing going on. I was coming to the main campus to eat one day. A cute brunette White girl approached me. She told me I was the prettiest Black girl she had ever seen. She started touching my face and asked did I want to come to her dorm. I was shocked by how bold she was. When I think about it now, I should have been insulted.

Unfortunately, I was eager to be with a woman, I was intrigued.

She then asked me if I knew any Black guys, because she said her roommates were looking to hook up. I figured I was single, and she was cute...for a white girl. Haha just kidding! I told her yes and called my home boys. They showed up and her and her friends turned up. They were giving head and having sex all over the room. I ended up fingering the girl and then I left. I was leaning more towards being with women at this point.

I was back at my dorm when I got a knock on the door. It was the guy from high school that was with my home girl in the lounge. I asked him what he wanted. He reeked of alcohol. He was stumbling and talking really fast. I told him he needed to leave. I told him there was no room for him and me to be together after what he did with my friend. He acted like he didn't know what I was talking about. He continued to beg for me to let him perform oral sex on me. He was on his knees holding onto my thighs. In a weird way I felt bad for him. I said ok. He pulled my shorts off so fast and went to it. He did it for a good while and then I stood up and bent over. We had sex that one time and I never accepted his calls again. I knew he was not someone I could make a life with.

I started talking to the guy that ghosted me again. His friends tried to set us up. We went on a few group dates. Then, on Valentine's Day he stayed the night.

Not long after that, we were riding with his friend. He pulled over in the rain and we got out. He asked me to be his girlfriend. I was not sure If I wanted to date him. I liked him, but I had a lot going on. He technically ghosted me when things got hard, and we weren't even dating. We were just friends, so I was weary. I was still healing, but I also did not want to keep sleeping with random guys.

I went out a few weeks later with my home girls. The girls I went to the party with were making shirts for the party. It was St. Patty's Day. They made one for me. The shirts had everyone's nicknames on them. I was wearing my shirt at the party when my home girl noticed something on the sleeve. They drew a small black penis on the fold of my sleeve, with the initials of the guy who raped me. My home girl told me to take it off and we got out of there. I wanted to fight. They thought my experience was a joke. I had not done anything to them and the hatred they had for me was real. I left her and anyone associated with her alone.

By this point I was over a lot. I was still working at the pharmacy. I was having trouble at home. I was being told I could not go out, but I had been living on my own for months. I told them I was moving out. I ended up running away at 18 years old. I stayed with my home girl and her family. They showed up at

152

my job and tried to make me go with them. They turned off my phone and told me I didn't have to come back. One day, not long after, I was working and my manager asked me a question. On the sales floor in front of another pharmacist he said..."

"Hey Journee, you said that player was pretty tall. That means he had a huge cock right?"

"He laughed at his statement. I was in shock. The other pharmacist spoke up for me immediately. I could not think of anything to say, so I left. I quit the job and started taking Xanax and Adderall. I was starting to drink a lot during this time as well. I was not sleeping much. I drank energy drinks to get by.

I got a job at the *YMCA,* and he worked at a furniture store. I had a great summer working and made some friends. I tried some great Caribbean food on the corner of Chili and Thurston, next to the spot I got my belly pierced. I was starting to model again.

I moved back on campus and into the dorm across the hall. I was starting to realize I wish he stayed in Casper mode. He lied about a lot. He did not go to my school or wasn't even in college. He did not have his own place; he lived with his sister. I even learned the phone he was using to talk to me was his sisters. I was already in too deep. His friend set up an opportunity for him to get a job at a group home. I was already working there and doing well. I had to dress this man while he was still sleeping, but he got the job.

We did not date long. We broke up after 7 months. I still let him stay because I knew he did not have a house.

I knew we would not be able to stay on campus forever. He was not supposed to be living there. I am sad to say I was desperate not to be alone. I decided I was going to move off campus and get an apartment. He had an eviction, so he could not rent. I told my program advisor my plans. He looked at me and said…"

"Remember when I said not everyone would finish? I knew you were not going to make it. If you leave this campus you will not graduate."

"I was devastated. He knew I was raped and had better grades the semester after. I was giving my all to keep going. I moved off campus. I had a car that I paid my mom for at this point. I was working and making all of my classes. He was rarely at the house and reminded me often that we were not together. That did not stop him from borrowing my car or money.

One night I was home studying. He went out with his friends with my car. They were all drinking, and he crashed my car into his friends. He said it was not that bad, but when they got there, as *Maury* would say, "that too was a lie." The front hood was bent back towards the windshield, and part of the light was damaged. I had to tell my mom I hit something. She was pissed and took the car. He didn't help pay for the damages or anything.

He ended up moving out to live with his friends. I was so mad at myself because I should have stayed on campus.

Of all times to leave me without a car and I was not on a bus route in the snow. I was not able to make it to campus for my finals. I failed the semester and did not get the funds to pay for my housing. On top of that, the girl I met that roomed with my friends from high school passed away suddenly. I was not even able to go to her funeral. I was losing grasp on everything fast.

"Journee, I think this would be a good time for another stretch and deep breathing exercise." Dr. Stone says standing up to stretch. Journee agrees and mimics her movements.

"Ok, I appreciate you doing that with me. Before we began speaking I just wanted to have that moment of calm. You just revealed a lot, and I know you are only halfway through your story. I am very sorry to hear about the sudden loss of your friend. I am not going to say I am sorry for you though. "I am sorry" is not sufficient for the way you have been treated. You carry yourself with such grace, and humility. I am deeply moved by your story.

I have been through a lot, but I have never met anyone like yourself. I have seen people complain about less and you hold your head up and face it. I am so proud of you. You should be proud of yourself too. Take a few more deep breaths and continue." Dr. Stone says sincerely with pen and notebook in hand.

"Thank you. I appreciate your care and concern. Ok, well after all of that, I ended up moving out of my first apartment. I moved to one that was closer to my family, without doing much research. When I moved in I learned it was infested with roaches. I was afraid to eat because they were only in the kitchen. My ex was nowhere to be found at this point. The cherry on top, I walk out one day and my car was gone. I thought it was stolen, but my mom had it. She took it because I missed a car insurance payment with her. She was teaching me a life lesson. I was so hurt. I stayed away from them for a while.

I started hanging with a new crowd. I went on a double date with a girl and two guys who were cousins. I started the date paired with one guy, but by the end of the day they told me we were switching. I guess they didn't hit it off. So, I started talking to the other guy. He told me that he couldn't wait to meet me, as if he knew me already. Then, he showed me his driver's license to prove his real name to me. I thought he was pretty cool, so we started talking on the phone. He had to go out of town for a while. We were listening to *Jodeci* and laughing on the phone when I heard a knock at my door. It was his cousin. He asked me what he was doing there. I told him I had no idea. He said to get rid of him. I felt like I was being set up.

I cracked the door to ask what he wanted, but didn't let him in. He was on some bs immediately.

He pushed his way in and said he wanted to talk. He said it was not fair that we had to switch and that he liked me on the date. He said the swap was not his idea. I told him that I really like his cousin and just got off the phone with him. I asked him to leave, but he sat down. He made a move to grab for me. I told him no, but I only had a tee shirt on and boy shorts. It made it easy for him to bend me over. It did not last long, because he could not keep it in. He said my vagina, "hurted" and that I was too tight. I thought to myself because you were not invited. He left and I called his cousin back. I told him what happened, and he was pissed.

He arrived back to town the next day. He came to see me. I could tell in his behavior that the energy had changed. There was no future for us. He only stayed there one night. We went on to become just friends.

I dated a couple guys at this time. I was not sleeping with all of them. I went on a date with a girl as well. But for whatever reason I was not ready to be in a relationship with a woman. I left everything in the apartment and started moving from place to place. Modeling and acting opportunities started to pick up. I would go down to New York City often on the *Amtrak Train*. I got to see *Bet's* show *106 & Park* be filmed.

One trip to New York City, I met some friends on set. We went to dinner and walked around *Time Square*.

We met some guys walking down the street. The girl I was with knew that I had a train to catch in a couple of hours. She offered to come with her to her house on Staten Island, but I thought that was too far. I did not want to risk missing my train. The guy I met offered to walk me to the train station. I agreed and said goodbye to my home girl. I spent the rest of the evening getting to know the guy. He seemed like a really cool person. We spent time together at a restaurant. After a few hours I was sitting in his lap. We kissed. He asked me did I wanna go for a walk to get ice cream. As we were walking, he asked me to step into a side alley with him.

The alleys that people sleep in on the ground and urinate in. I told him no, but he insisted. At first he was just kissing me, but then he started pulling on my pants. He was still trying to be romantic, but he was being too pushy. I gave in, and he leaned me up against the wall. No protection, he inserted himself into me on the street.

As we were walking to the train station. The route that he took had a stairwell. We were nowhere near the train station. He wanted to have sex. So, he sat on the stairs and told me to get on top of him. I did. When he finished inside of me I could feel my life leaving my body. I blame myself because I was flirting with him all night. I was sitting on his lap, we were kissing, but I was not expecting to have sex outside, standing in urine.

He ended up saying that he had to leave, but he would be back. I made it to the train station, and he never showed up. He never answered his phone again. I got on the train bawling my eyes out. A complete stranger came inside of me and then disappeared into the city night. I was convinced that I was pregnant and had contracted sexually transmitted diseases

When I got off the train I went straight to the Planned Parenthood and told them what happened. They tested me and gave me medication to help prevent STDs. I was still negative, but I had to come back a couple times to continue to check. At my next appointment I found out that I was pregnant. I was devastated.

I got a call from a woman. She was calling to let me know that the guy from NYC was reaching out to me. That he apologized for standing me up, and that he got arrested. She was his woman. She knew what happened and wanted to know if I was pregnant. I was so confused how she could have known. I told her yes, but I told her that he did not have to worry about me. She asked me if I was going to get rid of the baby. I told her no, and I didn't have to. I had another miscarriage. I was diagnosed with P.C.O.S. by this point" Journee takes a deep breath and pauses to reflect.

"I see that here on your medical paperwork, however you have two children. You are truly blessed. God has brought you through some dark valleys and carried you many times. I am so thankful you know the lord and still fight to this day. I want you to continue, because I look forward to seeing how all of this evolved into the amazingly strong and resilient Queen sitting in front of me!" Dr. Stone says with sincerity and pride.

"Thank you Alesha, you make me feel thankful I did not give up, and the moments I did, God brought me back up! Ok, well I was starting to party a lot. I was not coping with all of this well at all. I was still working hard though. I had switched around group homes a couple times. I was living with my ex now off and on. Staying with him and his siblings and sometimes at my parents. I started working at a particular group home, and I found out my exes ex worked there. He told me not to say anything to her about him. I told him that was weird, but he insisted. That did not end well.

Thankfully, we were in a good mood one night. He picked me up late, but it may have saved our lives. A car flipped from the other side of the highway and landed upside down in front of us. I ran immediately to help and pulled the boy out of the car. He got out to direct traffic. The next car behind the person who crashed was a fire fighter. The next car behind us was a girl who went to my college. God was working overtime. His car was destroyed, but he walked away with minor injuries.

I love helping people. I love working with people with disabilities. I had a special bond with all my residents. I swam with them, cooked for them, and took some to my family BBQ. My fondest memories was taking a resident to a *Carrie Underwood* Concert. We stood there crying singing *Temporary Home*. I heard he passed not long ago. I think of him every time I hear that song. My least favorite memory was working an overnight. I was doing a two person shift with a guy.

I did not have any issues with him prior to that day. He decided that he was going to pull his laptop out, turn on porn, then turn it towards me and ask if I liked what I was seeing. Like it was a candle commercial. I was disgusted and immediately worried it was going to go left. Most of my patients at the time were bed ridden. Right as my anxiety was going up, a resident that is ambulatory came out and sat on the sofa right between us. He quickly tried to get her to go to her room, but she refused. She stayed with me until the morning shift came. I never had to work with him again, thank God. She and I had a lot in common. People want to believe that people with disabilities are not aware of what is going on. They know exactly what is going on. I know that even if they cannot speak, they made an impact on my life forever." Journee says with tears in her eyes.

"That is beautiful about the concert. I love Carrie as well. I do not like what your coworker attempted to do. I am grateful that God sent you an angel in that resident in that moment. Please continue." Dr. Stone says tearing up as well.

I was still modeling at this time. My Homegirl I knew my whole life kept my hair fly for all of my shoots. I'd come up with the idea, and she would make it happen! My favorite was my mohawk with music notes shaved into the side of my head. My mom did not like that style as much as I did. Haha!

I met a guy on set of one of my shoots. He was cool and we started talking. The photographer was dating one of my coworkers. We were out at *Stoney Brook State* park shooting one day. I was doing an outfit change at the car. The photographer was fixing his lenses. My coworkers were waiting on us. He proceeds to pull his penis out of his pants, and gestures to ask if I like it. I went off. He tried to shush me. He put it away and we finished the shoot. I told her later and it ruined our friendship. It also ruined mine with the photographer. I was loving what we were doing, and he messed that up. I stopped shooting with him.

I met a guy out with friends. He had invited me to record some music. It was in a house. While he was showing me the studio room, he threw his head at my crotch. He was trying to pull my pants off and said he wanted to perform oral sex. I told him I had my period.

He told me to prove it. I showed him my pad, and he said well bend over then, that he just would not go down on me.

I told him no, and that was nasty, but he tried anyway. He could not get it to stay in, so he stopped. He cancelled my paid studio session, and I never got to record. I never went over there again. I told my coworker, and She told everyone at the job. They started bullying me. They put my name in a social media post, saying that "bitches like me," make it hard for good women.

I was so mad, I left the job and found a new job at *Highland Hospital.* I was born there, so it was cool to get hired. I was modeling still and working the night shift. I would learn quickly it was not as cool as I thought. I was on an overnight shift in the break room. My nurse manager came to see what I was doing. I showed her my modeling pictures. She said that they were not me, I thought she was joking. I laughed and said yes it is me. She then says to me..."

"Oh, I see what's wrong. You don't have those ugly black marks on your face in the pictures, like you do in person. Now get back to work!"

"I was so angry, because I was on break for one, and how rude is that. I had horrible cystic acne as a teen. I had to take *Accutane*, and it literally burned my face. My hyperpigmentation is something I struggle

163

with, and she so viciously attacked my pride in that moment. It would only get worse from there.

I found a new apartment in the *Lilac Festival* Area. I was talking to a few guys but was only sleeping with one. He was a cool person, but he had a lot of children and was older than me. I accepted that we were going to be just friends. I started to talk to a guy that I knew since middle school. Our other friend I was close to reintroduced us. We had been talking for a few months.

I went to his house for us to finally have sex. As we were doing it he was on top of me. It was feeling great, and then he made a statement that changed everything. He had not said anything prior, but at that moment he wanted to reveal he had HPV. I pushed him off of me and went to the hospital immediately. He did not give me the opportunity to choose. I never spoke to him again.

I was still hanging with my one home girl from high school. I thought we were tight. One night we went out. The guy who I went on the double date with needed a ride. We were friends by then, so I had no problem giving him one.

He was drunk and had to go to the bathroom. I pulled over and he got out. That is when she called me a Hoe. I was caught off guard, because it wasn't cute like in the movie *Love Jones* where she said..."

"You slept with him didn't you. You hoe! Slut puppy!"

"She was rude about it. She was judging based on seeing me with him and I was not. She said I was a selective hoe, but I was a Hoe. Like that doesn't even go together. I told her she did not know what she was talking about and that he was just a friend. She kept pushing and I told her she could get out of my car. He tried to calm us down, but that was the last time we went out.

Our friendship was never the same and we don't speak to this day. It hurt me for a long time. I was fighting to be a good woman. I wanted a man of my own. That situation with him was messed up, so when she called me that, it infuriated me.

I am a hoe?, because these dudes didn't have any self-control. I stayed at her house, and she stayed at mine. My grandma would make sure she made it home from work in the winter. She taught me so much. We used to get our sneakers together and name plate accessories! We were like Pam and Gina from the show *Martin*. I thought we would be tight for life, but in the end I felt judged and discarded.

I went out with my other homegirl from high school. I don't know how the most awkward double date occurred, but it was happening. I was on a date with my ex-from high schools best friend. The guy who subbed me for the girl at the dance. The same guy who she took to prom two years in a row. She was dating her new guy, who was my other home girls ex guy.

Messy. They drop him and I off. Somethings are just not meant to be. We were an example of that. I did not enjoy his company. He also lied to me and told me that my ex gave him permission to talk to me. I found out later from my ex that it was not true. I stopped talking to him and never saw him again. It all was just too much.

I started to hate everything around me. My ex was always late picking me up. I do not know why I let him drive my car. He asked me to pick his homeboy up one day. He takes a pass at me, then tells me not to say anything. Just to tell my ex a lie. I told him what happened, and he got mad at me. I was over all of them.

Things were getting worse at the hospital. I was working on a floor with very sick patients. I lost three patients in one day. It was devastating for me. I broke down crying. My head manager came to console me; she let me know that it was a part of the job and that I would have to get used to it. I could not get used to it. I was physically starting to breakdown. I had to go to the ER one night. I was waiting to be screened and saw my aunt being brought in. It was my aunt who was known for making pound cake. She passed away not too long after that.

The memory that stands out the most happened in a patients room. The patient was on oxygen and pulled it out of the wall, so the alarm is going off. I tried to get him to sit by reaching for his arm. He said to me..."

"Unhand me Nigger! I am going with him..."

He was pointing towards an empty bathroom. After he said it a second time, I told him that no one was there and turned to plug his oxygen back up. He fell flat to the floor. He did not say anything, he did not buckle. He just fell straight down. I pulled the button to call an emergency code. Everyone came rushing in. We got him up, and the doctor was deep in his thigh and could not find a pulse. They called his time of death right in front of me. I was so sad.

The last patient I lost woke up from a coma and spoke to me. He told me to tell his daughters he loved them. I got off shift and he passed away. I resigned not too long after.

I applied for a new job. It was a new group home. I got the job. I only had to pass the drug screening. That was no problem, but like always I put someone else ahead of me. I had a friend who went to school out of state. He had an important event at home and missed his way. He asked me to drive there to get him. I did. I was late getting back and missed my drug test. They do not give you another chance. So, I was without a job. I was at home one night with my friend.

I knew since middle school. We were playing video games. He had been a gentleman and never tried anything before. Unfortunately, that changed. He made a move on me.

I told him no and that I had a yeast infection. He said he did not care and pushed to perform oral sex on me. When he finished, I went into the bathroom. I had enough at that point. I took all the pills in my medicine cabinet and drank alcohol. I got down in the tub and prepared to die. I asked for forgiveness and felt myself slipping away.

I could hear him banging on the door, but I was slipping deeper into the tub. He broke open the door and pulled me soaking wet out of the tub. He rushed me to the hospital. I had to stay inpatient for a while. I saw other people there I knew too. My coworker from the group home came to see me. I told everyone I was in an accident, but she saw I was in the psych ward. She told everyone.

When I got out of the hospital a friend of the family offered for me to come to North Carolina to live. I accepted the offered and moved to the south. I was loving NC. I met new friends. I went on one movie date with a nice young man. I scared him away though. I told him some of my past and he seemed concerned. He asked me…"

"With all due respect, why does that keep happening to you?"

"He meant being raped or in a bad situation. I could not answer his question. I blamed myself for a lot of the moments, but some I could not avoid. I never spoke to him again. Not long after I met another guy. He was a musician. We met at the *Cook Out* restaurant. We talked on the phone for hours. I finally agreed to come to his house. I drove to the *YMCA* to have a swim, and then I went to see him. He was a complete gentleman, and we had sex. He made me his girlfriend on the spot.

He said he didn't want to leave room for anyone to bag me up. I enjoyed his company and accepted his invitation. I went home and was on a cloud. I was talking to my ex on the phone, but I was set on staying in NC. I started working for the opportunity to go to a *Keyshia Cole* concert. I was so excited. I went to hang with the son of my family friend. He had a few people over.

When I arrived, he suggested that I change, because they would be smoking. I had not done it in a while, so I was excited. We smoked and watched videos. It was good vibes. My family friend kept calling my phone. I knew I needed to get back to the house. I went to change, and he came in. We had flirted via text, but I had a boyfriend now and he was too close to the family. It would be messy, so I declined. He still kissed me and pushed for the moment. I attempted to lay back and let him get on top of me. The phone kept ringing, so I pushed him off to get it. I picked up and told her I was coming right away.

He tried to start again, but I insisted that we stop. I went to get off the bed and he stuck his fist in my ass. Literally, I am screaming and punching him. I am scratching him and begging him to stop. He finally does. He stands up. Kisses my forehead and said talk to me later, and walking into his bathroom to turn on his shower. I left his house running back to the house. Blood was running down my inner thigh. As soon as I came in, I told her what happened. She told me to go upstairs and to sit on a towel. I thought she was calling the police.

Instead, she called him, his mom, his dad, and her sister. She made me come downstairs and sit across from him not even an hour after it happened. She made us explain what happened. His dad asked him if I said stop. He got an attitude. His dad asked him again if I said stop. He said yes. That's when his dad said…"

"Well, that is rape, and Yo ass is going to jail."

"He jumped up and stormed out. The dad followed behind him. The mom then asked me what I wanted to do. I said go to the hospital. She said that was not a good idea. He and I just got off to a "bad start." That we should go to the concert together still.

170

They took my phone, made me wash, and made me stay at her sister's house while she was out of town.

I went everywhere with her. We went to a concert in the park and there were some legends performing. *New Edition*, and more. I stood there numb. I can barely remember hearing sounds.

One night she left her phone on the bed. I took it and hid in the closet. I called my aunt and told her I needed help. She said to hold on and that she would figure it out. I acted normal, but prayed she was coming. They made us go to the concert together. Same as before I was numb.

The memory that stands out most was when *Keyshia Cole* was coming on stage to perform, her stage crew messed up and almost hit her with the screen. She went off and left the stage. Everyone screamed for her to return. She did, and the concert was amazing. I cried the entire time. "I Remember," by *Keyshia Cole* hits different and always will.

On the ride back I lost it. I offered to give him oral sex. I wanted to get his DNA. I felt he did not deserve to be free. The way he did that, he was too confident. He must have sensed I was moving weird, because he was with it then he changed his mind. I let it go, and he dropped me off. Not long after my aunts friend came banging on the door. She demanded they let me come out. She picked me up and took me with her. I was so thankful for her. She took me to the hospital. They did a rape kit. The nurses were very kind. They took pictures and gave me medicines. After, she took me to the airport for my flight back to New York.

When I got back to Rochester, I was so happy to be home with my family. The case was dropped because I went to the concert with him. Despite being forced to. I ended up getting into an argument with my mom and I left again. I started staying with my ex and his family again. I would baby sit and help out. I was thankful for somewhere to be, but he would remind me often that we were not together. I was modeling, bartending, and event/ club promoting. We took a trip to NYC for a fashion show. When we got there they did not have rooms for us. I had a friend at the time I was talking to.

He worked at *B.B. Kings* club and restaurant in *Time Square*. He said we could stay at his house and could have his room. We had a good night dancing while he worked. I met a nice lawyer who brought us drinks. No one knew, but I would put cocaine in my juice at the time. I was afraid to put it in my nose. I did not drink when I used it. I let her turn up! My homegirl and I went to his house. He set her up in the room. I was saying thank you and he wanted to have sex of course. I was ok with it, because he was fine and he was letting us stay, but right before he ruined it. He said it would be dope if I could have both of us and I should ask her. I don't share dudes with my friends. Just because I am bisexual, it doesn't mean I am down

172

for everything. I took one for the team, so he would not try her. I bent over until he finished. I then went and laid in the room with her.

I took another trip to the city to film an episode of *HBOs Girls*. The guy that I met, that ghosted me because he got arrested, came to set to see me. He was in a completely different energy. He was polite and respectful. He came to wish me well and then he left. I never saw him again. That was one of my best trips to NYC.

The next trip to NYC I took, the African lawyer that I met invited me to come down. He paid for my way and everything. I was not used to that, because I was used to paying for everyone.

He had a really nice spot. The trip started off great! We had sex, and it was cool. Then, I asked to go and get food. He did not want to go. He gave me his key, money, and said I could go wherever. In the dark. Alone. Right! I left and rode the subway to Time Square. Which in NYC terms means I went too far! He called me and spazzed. I did not like the way he spoke to me. I told him to change my ticket to leave. He apologized, but I was done. I had no room to get into another abusive relationship. He kept messaging me, so I had to block him. I left the next day. I wandered and went to a movie until it was time to leave. I exchanged numbers with a cute movie worker and headed out. I started living with my ex and his family again. We were staying with his sister one night and they got into it.

She put us out. I was in the middle of drinking medical solution for a colonoscopy the next day. We went to social services, and they put us up in the *Cadillac Motel* downtown. Besides being one of the scariest hotels I have ever been in, I woke up to having pooped all in the bed and on him. Surprisingly, he was very understanding and helped me take a cold shower. The room had no hot water of course. He took me to my procedure, and we moved in with his mom. I was working at a new camp. The same *YMCA* I went to as a child briefly. My ex and I were not allowed to sleep in the same room.

He slept in the spare room, and I slept with his mom. I was grateful to have somewhere to stay. I was talking to a counselor that I worked with. He would give me rides to the house. One day he asked to come in to use the bathroom. I told him no; that it was not my house. He said it was an emergency. I was making this man drive almost 40 mins to drop me off. So, I let him come in…

He finished using the bathroom, and I was standing at the door to walk him out. He asked where I slept. I pointed at the room and told him he had to go. He kissed me. As good as it felt I told him that it was my exes' mom house, and we could not do anything. I told him we could get a room the following day. He did not want to wait. He kissed me and laid me back on the bed. I wanted him so bad, just not there. But it happened. I was so ashamed of myself. He left and I knew not to let him in again. I started looking for apartments that day. Good thing I did, because it is so true that what happens in the dark always comes to the light.

I came in from work and his mom asked me to talk. I was so worried, but I thought there was no way she could have known. Unless she had cameras. Nope, she had a condom in a Ziplock bag. She asked me where it came from. She said she found it on her dresser. He went to pull one out, but I am allergic to latex. He must have put it up on the table and it slid back. That is why you do not live foul. God will show you the errors of your ways. I denied it, but I knew I had to leave.

As if that was not enough, I had a run in with the past. The man my mother dated came to town. He asked to meet him for dinner. He wanted to discuss some education and business opportunities. I was looking for a good job, so I thought it was perfect timing. It was not. He took me to a hotel. He wanted to have sex. I could tell he was not as attracted to me as he once was. I had gained weight and cut my hair. He commented on both, but it didn't stop him. He was married. I asked what it meant, and he wanted me to be his secret. I lost it. I left and started emailing him hoping he would get caught. I feared for the women in his life. I told my mom and unfortunately she did not believe me right away. She said I was grown and wanted it. I can understand it sounded crazy, but it was true. I was so sad, because if I wanted it why would I tell her. I would never want to break her heart. I love her. We have healed since, thank God.

I needed a fresh start. I found a new apartment in Irondequoit. I was still working the club scene. I was talking to the guy I met on set and a few guys on the phone, but I was taking a break from sex. I had no problem being in the house alone. Thank God too, because my ex was outside watching a few times, to see who was over my house. Why I will never know since we were not together.

I went out and ran into the guy that I called for the random hookup with the white girl at school. He was drunk and asked for a ride home. He was so fine to me. He was dark chocolate and had curly hair. His lips were gorgeous. He invited me in. I accepted and we were in his room. He kissed me all over and it felt amazing. When he finished he got on top of me. At that moment, his nephew came downstairs. There was no way to lock the door. I was mortified. He yelled for him to go and wanted to continue, but it was over. I dipped out and never saw him again.

It was New Years Eve one night. I was at the club having fun. A friend of a friend came up and spoke to me. He was always cool. He asked me if I still liked girls. I said yes of course. He then said that his girl wanted to be with a woman, and he wanted to know was I interested. I told him yes, because when he pointed at her I thought she was so beautiful. I also confirmed it would be her and I only.

He said yes, that at most he would watch. He said that he would drive my car back to his house. Drop me off and then come back with her. I was drunk, so I did not mind not having to drive. We got to their house. He took me upstairs and showed me the room to wait for them. He left to go get her. I sat on the bed rocking back and forth with anxiety. I felt dumb. I was so excited about the girl, I set myself up for failure with him. Why didn't we all leave together? That's one reason I don't drink in public now and being drugged of course. I was worried, what if he did not come back, I didn't know where I was. What if she wants to fight me! As I am pondering it all, I hear them coming in. They are fighting...

She was beating his ass, asking whose car is it. I run and hid in the closet. They made their way to the bedroom. He pushed her onto the bed. She was fighting him to get off. Her hand was bleeding from punching the mirror. He was trying to kiss and calm her down. He was trying to get her pants off, but she kept fighting him. Before it went any further I came out of the closet. I told her that it was my car, and I was there for her.

She immediately came down and smiled at me. Thank God. She told me I was pretty. I told her she was gorgeous because she was to me. She had warm chocolate brown skin. She had full soft lips. Her eyes were big and bright through her glasses. Her smile was warm and inviting.

We were about the same height, but she was smaller in frame than me. She laughed and apologized to him. She started kissing me. I laid her back and started to perform oral sex on her. I had not done it before. Every time got messed up before. I was so excited. She seemed to really like it. I left them and never went back over there to be with him and her, but I stayed in connection with her.

During this time, I was going out a lot. I went out one night with my exes sister-in law. I ran into a guy I knew since high school. I always had a crush on him, but he was with the guy from high school that made me walk for not giving him head. The girls I was with decided to go with them. When we got back to the house I went inside to wait on the rest of the group. They came in and said the girls left. I ended up alone with 4 guys.

I had never been with multiple guys at the same time. They were ready to go. I was freaking out, then the jerk from school pulled out a camera. He started filming my face and saying my name. I told him to stop, that I knew I was going to be someone important one day and ran into the bathroom crying.

The other two guys saw I was crying and left immediately. The guy I liked came in to check on me. He made him delete it and told me I could go. When I got to my car the jerk from school had taken my money. I went back and banged on the door. I threatened to call the police, so he opened the door and threw my money in my face and closed the door. I was so angry.

I met up with the guy I liked twice after that. We spent time together one on one. I enjoyed his company, but the last time we both got too drunk. He passed out and I was sick in his bathroom. I had my home girl come get me and take me back to my exes sister's house. He was waiting with all my stuff in trash bags. He reminded me often that we were not together, but when I finally go out I am wrong. I stayed to myself for a while to avoid drama.

I took his nieces with me to the Puerto Rican Festival. I stopped by my old side boyfriend's house. He was back in town and had something for me. I was supposed to be pulling up quickly. He kissed me in the driveway in front of them. I was so mad because they thought my ex and I were together. That definitely was not the example I was trying to give. I stopped going places with his family.

I took a much-needed break to myself. I stopped talking to everyone.

I even checked into sex addiction therapy. I thought I had a problem and wanted to be better. I learned there that I had a "lack of weapon problem," some of the ladies said. They said I wanted to be loved and there is nothing wrong with that. The women in the group said that you are only addicted to sex if you are intentionally seeking those experiences. That if I was trying to casually date with no sex, and get to know someone, but it ends in sex that is not an addiction. It is rape, or I needed to learn how to draw clearer boundaries. I agreed. I never want to be a tease.

One woman shared in one trip out of town she slept with over 50 men, and she was financially affluent. She was not working as an escort; it was a competition between her and her home girls. I heard some stories while there that changed how I viewed myself. I was so grateful for their words, and bravery in sharing their stories. I was proud of the decisions I was trying to make. Even when I messed up, I acknowledged it and tried to be better.

I was talking to the guy I met on set. I was seeing him more often. I went out one night and my home girl tells me that she slept with him before. I had not had sex with him yet. I liked him a lot, but girl code comes first. I told her I liked him, but I would stop seeing him, but she told me it was ok and to do me. I asked her if she wanted to do it together. She said yes, so I invited them over.

We all were about to have sex. I went to perform oral sex on her, and she stopped me. She said she was only there for him. I told her that is not what we agreed to and asked them to leave. I was so mad. I started visiting with him on my own. We eventually had sex. We connected through creativity. I was starting to catch feelings, but he eventually broke things off with me. He told me that the other girl he was talking to was applying pressure. I respected his wishes and got out the way, but it hurt. I was buying him things and cut off anyone else I was talking to. As much time as we were spending together and the way we connected I thought I was applying pressure too. I was starting to think I was doomed to be alone forever. I was over Rochester.

I went out with a girl I knew from middle school a few times. We reconnected one night at the club. I approached her to say hello and noticed she was a little off. I got her out of the situation, and we found out she was drugged. I know God put me there for that reason. We hung out a few times. One night she got too drunk. I had to drive her home. Me and my ex and his brother helped get her to the door. When she realized they were there she told them they had to go, that her parents could not see them. How is it that they can get her home safely but weren't to be seen? I was starting to question our friendship. Then, she put the nail in the coffin. We went to go hang with her & her man. They had been talking for a while, so I thought it was dope.

When we got there she lets me know he has a roommate. The roommate is the cousin who ruined things for me with the other guy. I know I told her that story, so I felt set up. She went into the room with her man, and it left him and I. He wanted to talk. He let me know that he actually liked me and he doesn't like how things ended. We ended up having consensual sex. I realized after that we just did not have chemistry. I never saw him again after that.

As for her and me, I went off. I told her she was moving foul. That she was a hoe, for sport. She knew her parents would never accept her being with a black man, so she was sleeping with black men for fun. I was really trying to establish a life and marry one. Fighting to not catch a disease or be killed, and she thought it was a game. She did not like what I said, but she said I was right. Our friendship was never the same, and honestly in the long run I was ok with that. We served our purpose in each other's lives.

If things could not get worse. I went out with some home girls of mine from high school. I convinced them to go to my favorite club. They liked going to East Ave over St. Paul. I told them it was cool, and I took them on a Thursday, so it was not too crowded.

We had a great night until we ran into my big cousin. She had been dating my ex-boyfriend's roommate. I don't know what her issue was, but she started a fight with me.

I tried to walk away, but she followed us. I still tried to ignore her until she pushed my friend. That's when I swung. We were rolling around on the street. I heard a voice tell me to let go. I had her hair in my hand. I told them I wasn't letting go for shit. Then I heard a voice say they had something to make me let go. The police pepper sprayed me and slammed me on the hood of the car. I was being arrested. I had my friends take my car keys to call my ex to get my car and me. I was having an asthma attack by this point and gagging from how much he sprayed me. I went to jail overnight. He took so long I technically never bailed out. Thank God the judge saw that we were cousins and dropped the case. I haven't spoken to her since. I was losing faith in everyone around me...

I had a friend of mine from elementary school reach out to me. She said her cousin wanted to meet me. That he saw what I did in music and entertainment and wanted to have a meeting.

I met up with him at a restaurant and we discussed his goals. He kept it professional. I started working with him and his friends. I booked studio sessions and photoshoots. I booked club events and appearances. I was still working on my own music at the time as well. Like a dummy I even got a tattoo. I liked what the message stood for. I designed and got my own version. I felt safe with them.

I took a trip to NYC for a fitting. I brought my home boy who was in the show, his brother, my one home girl from church, and my home girl from my neighborhood. My one home girl had plans and met up with someone she knew. My other home girl and I were in the room with the brother. They were flirting the entire time, so I assumed they were about to have sex. I started getting ready to give them some space.

As I am leaving she calls me over. He tells me that she wants me but did not know how to say it. I told her not to play, because I really like girls. She pulled me in to kiss me. I was with it. I went to go pull her pants down and then she changed her mind. I immediately got up and left. Would you believe that she tried to tell my other home girl we raped her. After everything I have been through, she knew some of.

Why would I let anyone hurt her, let alone me? I went off. She apologized and said it was a misunderstanding. That was the most awkward ride back to Rochester.

I dropped them off and I never chilled with her again. The music guy asked me to come by his sister's house. I went and hung over there for a bit. I was not there long before he asked to use my car. I told him I could take him wherever he needed to go. He insisted he would be right back. I let him leave and immediately regretted it. He did not come back for days.

I mean days. He would not answer his phone, and I refused to leave without my car. I used that time to write a script. I had a deadline to meet, just to find out a jerk I knew was pretending to be an important producer. He was sending me fake emails. I had actors lined up and ready to rehearse, and he was playing with me the whole time. Of all times. Anyway, his sister was pissed. She let me stay, but I could tell she was mad. I found out later he had a woman and kids. He was using my car to go to them and hang in the streets. Things only got worse. He came back one night and told me we were having sex. We had not had sex before. I wanted to keep it professional. He said we were having sex one time only, and then he could not touch me anymore. I was so confused. I realized that I was in a deeper situation than I thought. He had sex with me and then he put me to work. We went to a house.

It was an escort service. They were preparing to sell me. I told them that I do not perform oral sex in real life, so I for damn sure wasn't about to for a stranger. The man said I was useless. He said I was too big, and said I didn't give head. He asked what he was supposed to do with me. Asshole told him to ignore me, and that I was down for whatever, but the man told him he doesn't make his girls do anything. His job was to protect. I spoke up and said I liked woman. He said he could make that work. I went on a few jobs. I would work, they would sit outside and then they would divide up my money.

I met up with an old man. He wanted to sit naked and drink wine. I met up with a few times an African man. He let me drive his car and was into buying gifts. We actually had sex, and it was good. I was shocked that he was paying for sex because he seemed like a good catch, but then I learned that he was a married business man. I went to the house of a young white man who changed his mind once I got there. He paid and let me leave. Then they sent me to a white woman's home. She wanted to be with a woman sexually.

She had paid previously, but the girls only gave her a massage. She proved her STD status, and I agreed to perform oral sex on her. She was married. Her husband was home but not supposed to come in the room. While I was in the room with her she started moaning out loudly. He told her to shut up. She put the pillow over her head. He then snuck in the room. He was trying to touch me as I was taking care of her. I fingered her with one hand while shooing and pushing him away. He finally left out. I went there a few times.

The last job that I went on I quit immediately. I told him he would have to kill me because I was not doing it anymore. We pulled up to the *Gates Motel* and walked up to the door. I knocked, but the person looked out the curtain and quickly closed it. He called the boss and said I could not come in, that he needed someone else. They asked him why and he said he knew me. That I knew his whole family and his girl. I was so mad that this person knew this about me, but I had no idea who they were. I was done!

I kept helping them with their music. I hosted a club event for him to perform. I set up VIP and a whole performance at one of the hottest clubs at the time. We got into it right before the show.

He was mad at the alcohol in the VIP. Mind you he did not pay for anything. He went off and called me a "Bitch," thankfully, his homeboy spoke up. He reminded him of how much I had done for them, and that they would not be having an event without me.

He told him to respect me. I was shocked, but grateful. I heard unfortunately he was killed a few years after I moved. We were driving around one day and decided to go to the beach.

His homie drove, he would sit passenger, and I was in the back, but it was my car. I told them I wanted to bring my girl. The girl from New Year's Eve. I had continued to talk to her. I was telling them how much I liked her. We picked her up and headed to the beach.

She started kissing me and gesturing for me to give her head right there. I told her we could wait. I had more respect for her than that. When we parked my home boy went to open her door. She grabbed at his pants to gesture she was going to give him head. He leaned and looked at me, like what the fuck!

I looked at him, like shit if that's what she wants to do. She started giving him head. Asshole got out and tried to come to my door, I told him to get away from me. I learned in that moment, once again, that girls can be just as cold as dudes. I had a fashion show in NYC, a few weeks later. I told him that I was going with my home boy.

He tried to get me to ride with him and leave my car. I told him no. I went to the fashion show, and it was amazing. I walked three sets at the *Greenhouse* in Soho. It was across the street from *Trump Soho* at the time. I was parked right out front. When we came out the door attendant came to tell me that my car had been hit. I could not drive it. We were supposed to be going right back, so we didn't have a room. My home girl from college thankfully let us come and stay at her house. We went to check the car and wait for insurance to get it, but when we got there it had been towed by the city. We left on the train.

He was so mad when I got back. He called me all out of my name. He told me I was worthless. I was glad it happened because it freed me…

My family was mad at me as well for messing up the car, but technically it was not my fault that someone hit me, but anyway. I had to go back to get my stuff out of my car at the tow yard in NYC. I took the train and then took a bus to the dock to get my things.

As I was walking back my suitcase burst open in the rain. All of my things fell on the ground. I wanted to step into the busy Manhattan Street. I took a deep breath and picked my stuff up. I kept walking and turned on Country Singer Gary Allan's song Every Storm (Runs Out Of Rain). I started walking and singing. The rain blended perfectly with my tears, but I kept going.

God sent an angel in the form of a bus driver. I was lost and cold. He was an older man from Brooklyn. He had his Yankee Hat on and his bus uniform. I was twenty one by this point. He was parked on the side and saw me. He was done for the day, so he let me on. I told him I was killing time before I left. He asked if he could take me on a date. Despite the difference in age, I respected the way he asked. I accepted and he ended his shift. We got into his car and our date began.

This man knew everything about New York City. The city is so beautiful at night. He brought me a hoodie! Then, he showed me *Madison Square Garden*, we ate gyros aka "street meat," and then we had a caricature portrait of us done. It was hilarious. It was an amazing date. Right as I got nervous, because it had to conclude. He dropped me off and was a complete

gentleman. He did not ask for anything and wished me well. I never saw him again.

When I got back I found out that I lost my apartment. I started staying with my home girl. She was such a dope person. She was comfortable enough to be nude in front of me. I noticed a few times, and as a bisexual woman I wanted to cover boundaries. I asked her if she was flirting or was I tripping. I told her I was bisexual. I let her know that we are friends and that was enough for me, but I also thought she was beautiful. She told me she was flattered, but she had not considered being with a woman. I left it at that, and we rocked on.

One night I was chilling on the sofa on the phone. I thought she was in the room by herself. She was not. The person she was having sex with comes out of the room with his penis out. She follows behind him with a robe on. I hung up the phone. I was immediately apologetic because I assumed they didn't know I came back.

However, they were coming to invite me to have sex with them. She misunderstood my offer. I was only offering to be with her. She was clearly drunk as well. I did not want her to decide something like that unless she was sober. I told them no thank you and dipped. I called our home girl to come and get me. She called the police. I told her she was being extra, and I had been through way worse before. It was all a misunderstanding, and I did not want to call.

She insisted and took me back there. The police arrived and knocked on her door. I was so mad. She came out looking so confused. The police explained what happened and she was in shock. The police asked me what I wanted to do, and I said nothing, because nothing happened. They left and I went off. She wanted to fight me for bringing the police to her door. I don't blame her. It looked like I called the police on her. We did not talk for a long time. I am grateful that we made up. We spoke like two grown women. We laid down all of our boundaries and guidelines to being present in each other's lives.

We both had grown so much. She met Royal and we became more like sisters. She was telling me she was having a hard time. We were working to get her some help, but unfortunately, she just passed away. I am having a very hard time with it…" Journee sighs, as her eyes fill with tears.

"I am very sorry to hear about the loss of your sister. To lose another friend so close to you so young is hard. I know that they are watching over you! Please continue." Dr. Stone says handing Journee a tissue.

"Thank you. I call them my Girlfriend's in the sky! Ok, where was I? I continued to date. I was taking my time. I would only talk on the phone. I had been swindled at this point and worse. I had a guy on the first date ask me to pay his phone bill, and then he never paid me back. I was so glad we did not have sex. I went on another date that went well but ended the same night. This fine chocolate man took me on a date to *Niagara Falls*. I drove. He wore all white and had white forces on. He was clean. His teeth were perfect, and so was his skin.

He smelled amazing. We had a great time at the casino. Then, I went to drop him off. He asked me did I want to come inside. As fine as he was, I knew what could, and after our date probably should happen, but I was not ready. Plus, I was still "sus" on his occupation. Haha. He respectfully accepted, got out, and I never saw him again.

I went on a date with a guy I met at the club. He was a complete gentleman. We drove the same car. He respected that I did not mind driving myself. He took me out to a bar. I had not been there before. It was nice. I saw family that I had not seen in a while. I realized it was the mature, grown, and sexy spot. I wasn't mad. I loved places like that. I used to go out with my ex's sister to a bar out in the suburbs for Halloween. It was always good vibes.

Anyway, we were at the bar, and it was going well. Then, his cousin got into a fight. The other person pulled a gun on him, and I was out. I got in my car and called my home boy frantic. The cousin that we decided to just be friends. He told me to come to him.

I managed to drive to him. I stayed the night. The next morning, I was dropping them off and in front of his friend he says…"

"I didn't eat your pussy, because I didn't know where you had been!"

"I was so embarrassed and angry. Why would you say something like that, in front of someone, and were supposed to be friends? The other guy joked, as fine as I was he would have. He even dissed him, and said that's why he had bumps on his face. I was even more offended. It was a blessing I did not have something. A lot of people that I knew did. He thought that he was so cool because he was an "asshole." I didn't ask him to eat my pussy. I never judged him for where he's been. I came to him in a moment of genuine concern. I learned then that we were not friends. I stopped speaking to him. We remained cordial, but it would never be the same.

I stayed in the house for a while. I finally went to the mall one day. I felt like being silly, so I wore my little sister's blue wig from spirit day. I met a cute guy. He was tall and caramel brown skinned. He had hazel eyes and a nice smile. We exchanged numbers and talked on the phone a little.

I finally went out to the club. I had been low for a while. I ran into my ex's brother. I went to speak and hug him, but he stopped me immediately. I was taken back, but I stepped back to address the issue. He told me he was good on me. I asked what he meant. He said that he knew all about me and that I could do what I want, but just not while I was fucking his brother. I told him we have been broken up for years, and that technically we just deal with each other off and on. I let him know I was single. He apologized and said he was not aware of our arrangement.

I took a trip to NYC for an all-white yacht party. I was there visiting the guy I met at the movies. He was my date for the event. I had a great time. We were all at the restaurant in Time Square after when I got a phone call. It was my ex calling to tell me that his brother had passed away.

He didn't say much and then hung up. I was so worried. I rushed home to help with the funeral. I found the photo they used for his obituary. I had to hold his daughter at the casket and explain why her daddy was sleeping. That was one of the hardest things I have ever done.

I found out that the movie guy had a girl, so I never spoke to him again. A few weeks after all of that, a friend of the family was killed. His funeral was so sad. Everyone was hurting. I started seeing the guy from the mall. We started hanging out daily. We went to get tested together. He let me know that his family was strict.

That we could not be in the room unless we were serious. I had no problem waiting and respected

194

his wishes. I actually really appreciated it. I was getting to know his family one day. We were all talking in the living room when I noticed an obituary. It was the same man that I cared for, that told me to tell his daughters he loved them. His mom was the daughter. I got chills. She cried so hard. He was in shock. I thought it was all fate.

I had enrolled in school again. *Monroe Community College*. I was majoring in film. I landed a spot to have my own campus radio show. I was going to be the host of a Country, and Hip Hop, R & B show. I was loving my classes. I was attending church with his family and preparing to be baptized. He proposed to me. I accepted. It was moving fast, but I was trusting the Lord.

I began taking vocal lessons with my ex's brother-in-law. I knew him since I was a little girl in church choir. I was excited about the lessons. I had been writing music, but I wanted to learn how to sing properly.

He had me come to the studio. He showed me a few breathing techniques that involved touching my stomach to show me my diaphragm. I left and scheduled for future sessions. Then, he tried to slide in my DM. I told my ex immediately, He told me to block him, before he had to kill both of us. I feel that did not need to be said, but I blocked him and did not have any more lessons. My ex asked about me being engaged and I told him I was happy, because at the time I was. One night my fiancé and his family got into an argument. I intervened and felt the Lord speaking through me to them.

I left them all crying in a prayer circle. I felt like I finally found my purpose and my place. It came time for me to go and be baptized. He was in a bad mood of course. I was starting to see he was not a positive person. He said he wasn't going, and I should reschedule. I did not want to reschedule. I asked his dad if he would take me. He said yes. I got baptized. I had done it before growing up, but this time felt different. I saw a beautiful blue sky and fields of grass. It was the perfect temperature. I felt like I was there forever, and then they pulled me up. I felt changed.

I drove home that night singing *"If I Die Young"* by *The Band Perry*. That song in that moment was therapeutic. I had once been suicidal, now I was living in peace. I was prepared. If my moment were to come I no longer had to be afraid. What I saw changed my life and I was fully committed. My college roommate and sister from the college summer program passed away on that same night, one year later. Which was actually the night I met Royal, but we will get to that.

Ok, so back to my fiancé. It was his birthday. My uncle let me borrow his *PlayStation* to bring over for us to play. We were chilling in his room when he got into it with his mom. I told him that he was being disrespectful to her. He told me to shut up and slammed the door shut. I could hear them yelling, so I started looking up the bus route. Thank God something said let me pack up my uncles game. I was sitting on the bed with my bookbag ready to go. He comes in the room and locks it behind him. He saw that I was on the phone to leave, so he snatched it out of my hand. As he did he scratched my face. I could see I was bleeding. I freaked out. I started screaming give me my phone, so his parents would hear us. He slammed me up against the window. I heard it crack, and we almost went out the second story. I pushed him back to get off the window. He slammed me on the bed and started pulling my pants off. I told him to stop and started kicking him. He was reaching for my underwear when his dad bust in. He yelled to ask what he was doing. I jumped up and ran past them, I yelled out to him that he knew I had been raped before, and he would do me like this.

I took off running down the street barefoot. He was chasing me in the dark. He lived not too far from that same corner of Thurston and Chili. I ran across the street dodging cars. I almost made it to the other side when I heard someone yell out..."

"Hurry up, you're about to get hit by the bus!

"They were right, I looked up and a RTS bus was coming right towards me. I jumped on the curb, just making it, The buses wind blew my hair. When I looked up he was still coming. I stumbled into the liquor store. I fell into the display; They yelled for me to get out of there with that bs.

As they were guiding me out, the person noticed the poster on the wall. It was me. I was sitting center of a poster for my upcoming fashion show. It was going to be on my grandma's birthday, so seeing that date, my family was all I could think about. He said wait; that's her. The vibe changed, and now I was worthy of help. The dudes got at him to get away from me. Thankfully, a woman was walking by and saw it. She called the police for me and told them what happened. Then, she called my ex for me. Despite us not being together and everything we had been through, he showed up and fast. He took me back to meet the police and get my phone. The police told me that if I wanted to press charges, that I would have to be arrested as well, because he said I hit him.

I put my hands out to be arrested, but my ex slapped them down. He asked if there was another way. The officer told me to file a restraining order. We left. He took me to my parents' house. I told them what happened, and they got annoyed with me.

My mom asked where her brother's system was. I told her I made sure to get it, in the midst of getting my ass beat. I told them I was going to get the order, but they told me to let it go. I did. I knew it wasn't going to get better, so we left. He took me to a hotel. I tried to let it go and move on. I blocked his number, and social media. I went back to school. I was doing well in my classes and was not letting this stop me. I got to campus one day, and he was waiting for me. I went the other way, but he grabbed my arm. I tried to pull away, but he pushed me up against the wall. He said he just wanted to talk to me, and I was not being fair. He said that people fight, but I did not let him apologize. I told him I had been through enough, and to leave me alone. As I was running the other way, I ran right into security. They saw the entire interaction on the camera. They told me to come with them, and they escorted him off the campus. I filed for the restraining order. My home girl came with me and his parents with him. In court he said to give me whatever I want, and he would leave me alone. After I saw him once at *Cobbs Hill*, he left immediately.

My ex invited me to a Ted Shuttlesworth event with his family at their church. I was shocked they still welcomed me to come. They definitely showed me what having faith in something no matter what others around you believe in.

Your character and choices are what secures your seat on the other side, not someone else's choices. I have been to a lot of church services, but this event changed my life. I have seen people catch the holy spirit, but I had not experienced anything like this before. I was listening to the service, and at first it felt like everything he said, from numbers or places, all related to my life. Then I felt myself starting to rock. It progressed to I had to stand.

My ex's mom was so calm, as if she knew exactly what was happening. I no longer felt in control of my body, but I was not afraid. I knew exactly where I was. I went to excuse myself to get out the pew. My ex tried to grab me, but it was too late. I walked to the front of the church and sat right in front of this man.

An usher came and told me the area was reserved and that I had to move. I told him I couldn't move. I genuinely could not feel my legs. He asked me to move again. I told him that God told me that I could sit there. He went to pull my arm, and the speaker told him to let me be. That I could sit there. I was now rocking on the front pew. It was empty.

When he finished speaking he called me up. He spoke over me. He said that something took over me, that made him have to see me. He told me that all the pain would stop. The bleeding that I thought I caused would be removed from my body.

I had been bleeding for weeks at that point, and did not know why. He touched my stomach and then my forehead and I felt a force over me. I turned and faced the door. I walked out the back of the church and walked down the side of a busy road to the hospital. I checked myself in because I thought I had gone crazy. I found out then that the stuff I was smoking with my ex-fiancé that I had the restraining order on was laced. It is a miracle I survived. I know that the experiences that I had with the Lord were real. God humbled me in front of my ex's family, and other classmates of mine were a witness. I accepted my wrongs and released them all that day.

I got one last apartment before I moved. I lived off of Park Ave. I loved my apartment. I was only hanging with woman at this point. I had a home girl who would take me to the reggae spots. I had another home girl I would chill, smoke, and ride out with. I also started talking to the girl I met during the threesome. She would spend the day with me. We would walk to get food. Then, we would come back, smoke, drink, and make love to each other all day. I loved being with her. I was still allowing my ex to hold space in my closet, so I felt like I was hiding her. I also had to hide that I smoked. I hated that. Well, all of that changed one night. He came home and her and I were there. It was his birthday. She asked if we should give him a threesome. I told her yes. We could tell he was nervous. We led the way, and it turned out well.

He still was set on that we were not together. I knew I deserved better, but I was so afraid to be alone. He would borrow money, to go hang with his and my old friends at a restaurant in view of my window. When I ask to come, he would say his friends did not like me, so why would I come? The girl from school I called a hoe for sport was one of the people there. I was over it. One day I went through his phone while he was in the shower. I paid for it at the time.

He had pictures on the screen and a girl saying she could not wait to see him. I knew he stopped letting me come to his job with him. I flipped out on him. He tried to grab the phone and pushed me back.

I got up and started punching him. I kept hitting him in the face. He did not hit me back. He went to my window and pulled the screen back and threatened to jump out. At that moment I moved out of his way. His sister called me and said I did not have to do him like that. She was right. I was not living right. I was losing it. I looked a mess to everyone around me because it was always something going on. I needed a new start.

I knew then I had to leave. I found a school named *Full Sail University* in Orlando, Florida. I applied, got accepted, and found an apartment walking distance to campus. I found someone to sublet my apartment, and I said my goodbyes. My ex drove me to the airport, and we said our final goodbye.

"Journee. I commend you. It was brave of you to leave your home, to go to a new place, because you wanted better for yourself. A LOT happened to you in a small period of time. There was no way to heal from anything because more incidents occurred. You needed a reset. I have so many things that I want to show you. Help you heal and grow. You made it to this point with not a lot of resources. You trusted God and it shows. I am proud of you. We will now discuss your move to Florida and then meeting your husband." Dr. Stone says eagerly!

Chapter 8

"New City, Same Game."

8

"Ok, lets discuss your move to Florida, and how that went. I am ready." Dr. Stone says with her pen and notebook in hand.

"I arrived at the Florida airport. wearing corduroy pants in 85 degree weather. My home boy from middle school was there to pick me up. He went to school there and worked in the clubs. I appreciated the tour and ride to the house. I stopped and got a few things at Walmart, and then he dropped me off.

I loved my new apartment. It was nothing fancy, but it was mine. It was huge. I had a large one bedroom, and one bathroom. I had a king size bed and still had room. I did not have a living room set yet, but it was just me. I sat on my bed.

I got familiar with the area by walking. I did not have a car, so I walked everywhere. I quickly started dropping the weight I gained. I walked to a new church and Walmart to get my groceries. The lizards being everywhere took some getting used to.

I went to campus to start orientation. As soon as I walked in I saw a guy spot me. He was cute, but I did not like his hair. He approached me and asked if I was lost. I told him no; I was there for orientation. He showed me around and introduced me to his friends. I met some other classmates at the event. I became friends with a few girls and guys. We had a huge freestyle cypher. It was a great icebreaker.

I started classes. I started promoting events right away. I got linked in and threw a big mixtape release party. I was making a name for myself in a good way. I loved our school. Everyone was doing something. We were all from all over. There was so much creativity.

I finally had the guy from orientation over. We had been hanging a lot on campus. He came to spend the night. We had sex. I was sure he was going to be my man. I was not leaving room for anyone else, but he did. He had a girlfriend. She lived back in his hometown. I found out she was arriving to a party at his house. I was there and he told me minutes before she got there. I met her and then my girls and I left.

I met another guy on campus. He was cool. I met his mom. She was there helping him set up. She taught me some cool things in a small time. He started driving me to school and making sure I got groceries and weed! I was holding out on sex, because I did not want to if it was not going anywhere.

I hosted an event at my house. I filmed a short film for a woman's film festival. My film was about sexual assault. I had some guys show up to support but would not act out scenes showing those behaviors. I respected that. They also gave me a machete to protect myself.

I had a get together at my apartment. I had a few classmates over. When it was winding down, one guy stayed back. He had been flirting all night. He followed me into my room. He sat on my bed. I sat on the floor, I explained I don't let people in my bed with street clothes on. He did not move. I told him straight up I was not having sex with him. I was waiting for a relationship. He said he did not want one and only wanted to fuck.

I got up and went to the bathroom. I could feel where it was going. He came and pulled on the handle. I am glad it was locked. I called my friend who was a Marine. He was on a date. I asked them to come over and create a diversion. He showed up with his date. I was so grateful. He pretended we had a project, and I forgot they were coming. He tried to tell me to get rid of them. I told him I had to work on the project, but they could give him a ride home. They did and then offered for me to stay with them for the night. I appreciated them making sure I was safe.

I threw a big party after. I saw my husband there, but we did not get introduced that night. I had my home girl over. She invited the guys. It was the person I went out of my way to get rid of. I knew he had a girlfriend. I saw it online. He flirted with me all day. I told him that I was good on him. My home girl thought it was funny, and I was just playing hard to get. They pushed him and I into the bathroom and held the door. He of course made his move. He told me to get in the shower. He tried to put it in from the back but could not. He stormed out of the bathroom. I stopped dealing with him completely after that. I was stuck with the girl for a little longer.

A few days later someone tried to break into my apartment. Thank God I had alarms. I saw a dark hooded figure running down the steps. I called the police, and they never came. I called my home boy, and he came immediately. He told me I could stay with him. I slept in his bed, and he slept in the living room. Conveniently, one of the girls I met and had been hanging with claimed she was having issues with her roommate. She "needed" somewhere to stay. She asked if she could stay with us. He said yes. I was so mad. She slept out there with him, and not in the room with me.

One night she comes back to the room and asked me did I want to have a threesome with them. Mind you she said she did not like woman. I told her she was tripping, that I had not even had sex with him yet. She tells me they just had sex. I was infuriated. I actually liked this person. She said he was ugly.

He came back there like a scared puppy. He said she made the move on him and thought I would be with it. I believed him because she was sneaky. I had unfortunately signed a lease to be roommates, and she pulled this before we moved in.

When we moved, we agreed no one from the past at our new place. She not only invited everyone still, but I came out to get a drink and she was riding him with the door open. She wanted me to be jealous clearly. I was not. I was disgusted by both of them.

One night she makes a move on me. I was thrown completely off. I was barely her friend by this point. She shared more of her back story, and that she had been through trauma as well. One thing led to another, and we had sex.

I crossed paths with my husband on the stairs leaving a party. He spoke but kept it moving. I thought he was so handsome. I learned later we were hanging with the same crew, but at different times.

We had a home girl come over one day. She was frantic. She said our homeboy had beaten her. I immediately got ready to run down on him. I was promoting events with him. She said he broke her glasses, and everything. We were all on her side, until she took his call on the porch. It was weird, so for my own protection I started filming what she was saying. Come to find out she was making it all up. When I confronted him, he said she was lying. It caused a big mess and divided me from the group.

We all had a "makeup" night. They invited us to their house for drinks. I tried a few drugs at this point, but not molly. It was crazy, and like *Trinidad James* said, I definitely was sweating! Some people were happy, and others were crying. It was too much for me and made me feel very sexual. I got out of there and called the guy I used to talk to. He showed up, but he refused to do anything. He said I was too far gone and need to just get some sleep. He was right. I thought I was going to die. My heart was racing and drinking water made it worse.

After that, I was keeping to myself. I did not want to date anyone. My roommate started dating a guy from a new crew. She invited them over, and my husband was one of the guys. My heart dropped. I was not dressed for company that was actually cute. I stayed in chill clothes to give the vibes I was not interested. Now I wanted to change, but it was too late. He came and sat next to me. I know now that was him making a move. I am so glad he did. We talked all night, and he sealed his fate when he knew who *Kenny Chesney* was ha-ha! They had to leave in a rush before the pizza came. I was so sad.

A few days later I was running my mouth. Saying how much I liked my husband to my home girls. I was running my mouth and clowning around about what I would do to him. I was going in! I thought it was just the girls, but his home boy was in the room.

He came out and said he could call him. My stomach dropped. I was so embarrassed and told him it was ok.

He told him anyway and eventually my husband text me! That is where it all began for him and I." Journee says with a big smile.

"Journee, thank you. Thank you for sharing your story with me. I was recording everything. We will be going over all of these events in our future sessions, but I need you to know now that you are brave. You are a good person. Let go of a lot of the guilt and shame you carry. I know you have to take accountability for the role you played. However, you were misled and forced by a lot of people. Rape is not just a stranger on the street slamming you down. Its touch, kiss, any contact after you said no. You can "give in," but that is out of fear or accepting that this was a normal behavior. It is not. A real man, or woman would wait. They would have patience and understanding. They would have self-control and respect for themselves. Regardless of what they thought of you. They need to love themselves more. I am so proud of you for taking your healing seriously.

You are a mother and a wife now. You have always mattered, but being a mother is the most important job you will ever have. Death is your retirement plan, because while you're living they are your priority and responsibility. For life, not just until they are 18. You need to lead them with your husband leading y'all under God. If you keep God first, everything else will fall into place.

I trust and believe you know that though. Your faith is what got you to this point and I am so thankful to witness that. We will take a small break; I have to adjust my schedule to add one more hour block to our session. I want to get your process done today, so we can start your treatment plan this week. When we come back we will discuss your journey with your husband and how you became the powerhouse couple and amazing family you are today!" Dr. Stone says giving Journee a high five as she exits the room.

CHAPTER 9

"Love in a hopeless place..."

9

When Journee met her husband, it changed her life forever. Their friendship, relationship, and journey would be nothing like she dreamt growing up. It would be far greater and definitely worth it…

"Ok, just know that our love story has been a rollercoaster. We have been through a lot, but God has been good the whole way. I thought I left no room for someone to be able to get close to my heart again, but I was in too deep at that point. I got a text message saying…"

(Text message):

"Hey this is Royal. My boy said to hit you up. How are you doing?"

"I almost threw my phone. I went running out screaming at my roommates. I was mad, but I wasn't mad. I really liked him and wanted to get to know him.

We talked for a few days and then he came over to see me. This man walked from his apartment to mine to see me. I could not believe this man walked to see me. I knew I was cooking for him! Haha.

When he arrived he had on a pair of shorts that he made from his old *Army ACUs,* showing off his strong well-oiled legs in the Florida sun. He was 6 feet tall and still had his Military close cut at the time. He wore long white socks. I had never seen a guy be as fresh as him wearing high socks. He was just different.

He was a complete gentleman. We took a cab for our date at *Denny's,* my choice at the time, he informed me they do *Waffle House* in the south! He won me a stuffed animal from the claw machine. I still have it! When we got back to the house we talked and laughed all night. We text about a lot before he came, so a lot had been discussed already. He kept it so real with me, I was even more intrigued by him. He explained that he was separated and was getting a divorce. He told me that he was talking to more than one woman, but he got tested often.

We smoked and had a few drinks. He provided everything to keep the party going! He taught me a new phrase that he used when he felt good, "Jazzy." I loved it and have been saying it since. We had an amazing evening, and he clearly was going to stay the night.

He asked to take a shower. I thought that was so sexy. I had taken three before he arrived. I was so nervous, I just kept getting in! I could smell his shower from the room. He brought his own body wash. He smelled amazing. I was so excited because a man can be fine as hell, and his scent or body odor can ruin it all. This man took good care of himself, and it showed. He came out in his black boxer briefs, and I was able to see how in shape he was. His hot cocoa brown skin glistened in the moonlight shining through my window. The vibe was everything.

He gave me a massage and then laid me on my back. Lets just say he changed my view on sex forever. Best I ever had is an understatement. It was his confidence, but not arrogance. It was his care and concern for my body. His body and size was naturally intimidating, but the way he handled me left me on a cloud. He knew some of my past experiences at this point and he made me feel safe. I enjoyed him so much he never left. I guess that means he enjoyed my company too!

We prepared for Thanksgiving. By this point this man brought me new clothes and shoes. He even brought one of my home girls some clothes, because he knew we did not have much at the time. His mom had just passed away. This would be his first Thanksgiving without her. He told me she was a great cook, and that he missed her a lot. I cooked an entire Thanksgiving spread in two pots and two aluminum pans for this man and our friends. He tells people to this day that meal is what sealed the deal for him, that with me being from up north and cooking like that made me different. He made me his girl. We agreed that we would continue to enjoy the company of women if it presented itself. I was cool with that as an option. My roommate cost us our apartment, so we started staying with our homegirls.

I would spend some days at Royal's house as well. I left my phone at my homegirls while I was there once, and my phone "magically disappeared," I lost all of my contacts, but Royal got me a new *iPhone* that same day. It had the cutest *Hello Kitty* Case on it. He was serious about taking care of me and making me feel appreciated. I appreciated his efforts and his actions matching his words.

One night we had a date set up with a woman. Royal knew her before me. His roommate met her online but decided to move on to another girl. He said ok, so Royal and her started talking. They started hanging on their own at her house. He slept with her and her two home girls in a consensual orgy. I was turned on by his honesty and confidence to please more than one woman. Royal had class that day. He sent her to come and pick me up. We were supposed to get to know each other and then we would pick him up after his class.

Her name was Sunshine, and it fit her perfectly. She was so pretty to me. I could see why he liked her. She was petite. She was shorter than me. She had honey blonde and brown highlights in her hair. It was cutely curled into a short cut, like a caramel *Marilyn Monroe*. She had full rosy lips and a laugh that made the hairs on my neck stand up. In a good way. I liked her right away. We liked each other. We went to hang at my home girls house because that was where I was staying. I hung with her, my old roommate, my home girl, until Royal was ready.

We went to pick him up. I went to get out to get in the back, but he insisted I stay. He got in the back. He greeted us and spoke kindly to both of us. He was grateful and happy to see that we were hitting it off so well. We drove back to my home girls place to chill for the rest of the night. When we got there my home girls other roommate was back. They had her tell us we were not welcome and closed the door in our face. I was so embarrassed and pissed. I paid to be there, and all of my things were inside. I told Royal and Sunshine to wait in the car. I went back to see what the problem was. I decided to leave with Royal and Sunshine. As I was leaving my old roommate followed me out. She put her hands around my neck and said she wanted to come. She had been shady and knew Royal did not like her. She slept with his friend. I pulled her arms down and told her no. She has hated me since.

I actually got into it online with her not too long ago. Before we had kids. She tried to make fun of us for being homeless, forgetting we were homeless together. I came back with point for point and then I guess I took it too far. She has had me blocked to this day. Anyway, we decided to go back to Royal's place. We smoked and had some drinks. He went to get more, and Sunshine kissed me while he stepped out. She then set the mood and tone for the evening. She put my hand on her vagina and told me to feel how I made her feel kissing her. I was so turned on by her.

There was no denying that I liked woman at this point. Royal joined us not long after. He connected with me while I connected with her and vice versa. We were all in a vibe together. I had never experienced a threesome like that one. We all laugh that it was dust, but the room felt like it was sparkling in the moonlight.

We heard a car pull up. It was Royal's roommate. Royal went to get us more drinks and speak to him. Everything in me said to get dressed, and I told Sunshine to as well. We were putting our clothes on when Royal came back in the room. He said it was good that we were getting dressed, and his roommate was tripping about Sunshine being there. I was confused. I was just ready to get out of there.

As we are wrapping up this man kicks the door in with a knife in his hand. Royal immediately approached to defend us. The man started yelling at Sunshine. He said he told her to never come back. That was news to us clearly. He let us leave. We got to the car and Sunshine was shaking. I told her to get passenger side and leave the door and the trunk open. She begged me not to go inside, and to just leave. I reminded her that Royal was literally just inside both of us and you would leave him with a man with a knife out… I went inside hoping she would be there when we returned.

I went back inside and asked if you could have seen the look on both of their faces. They could not believe I came back. His roommate yelled for me to leave, and I said I was coming for my stuff. He tried to call me out my name, but I ignored him. Royal got us safely to the car and we left. I got my things from my home girls house. They kept apologizing for making us leave. We stayed in hotels for a few weeks. Finally, my home girl agreed to leave with us and go to NC with Royal.

We lived with his best friend he calls his brother and his wife and their three children. Speaking of children. Royal and I had just found out we were pregnant. I got to meet Royal's dad. Its so funny looking back, because that's Papa now, but he has been a genuinely good person since the moment I met him. I enjoyed living in North Carolina, but we needed our own space asap.

I started looking for jobs and couldn't even get hired at *McDonald's*. I was not doing well in the southern job market, not getting hired was new for me. I ended up having to go to the hospital. I had a miscarriage. They did a procedure for this pregnancy, and it was painful. My home girl was with me. They would not let Royal back there, because we were not married. He hated that. Not long after I got out, my home girl decided to leave. She didn't tell us, in the middle of the night her family pulled up like we were holding her. I know damn well she knew they were coming from hours away.

Things were ok once she left. We had more space and less resources being used. We worked together as a family. One friend of his, however, was anything but family.

I was babysitting nephew at the house while the guys went to record some music. He and I were alone when a knock came at the door. It was Royal's other home boy. I never got good vibes from him, and I was not wrong. He made a move to touch me. I told him to get away from me. Even nephew pushed his head when he tried to lay on me. He was drunk and had his gun in his hand. He was saying all these horrible things about Royal and trying to get me to flip sides. I picked the baby up and went in the room and locked the door. He came and tried to open it. I looked at the window and nephew looked at me. For a one year old to not be crying during all of this. His face said he was trying to help. As we got ready to go out the window, I heard him go out the back door. I quickly ran out the front door with the baby in my arms. At that moment Royal was walking back up the street. He said he noticed ol boy hadn't made it to the studio and something said come check on us. I was so glad he did.

We started to move around a lot. We moved to Richmond and Norfolk Virginia.

I got my dream job at *Victoria Secret*. I loved my job and was doing well at work. We started treatments to help us conceive. After our first miscarriage I was told we would not have any children. Royal never accepted that or let me. He said God had final say. He was so right.

Our Pastor said the same thing. We went home for my grandma's birthday. She wanted all of us to go to church. We filled the pews for her! Pastor spoke about the story of Sarah. Her faith led her to become a mother. After service I got to introduce him to Royal. He was so excited. He told stories of me as a little girl. Then he asked about our children. We told him, not yet. He said do not worry at all. He prayed over us and said that the next time he saw us, that we would have children. He unfortunately passed during the pandemic, so we did not make it home to see him. However, he was right. We had two amazing daughters right before he passed away. God is good. That is why we named them after all of our angels, and family we love!

So, I found out I was pregnant. I was 8 weeks. It was really going to happen. Then I started to hurt. We went to the ER. I had an I.V. in my arm and fluids running. My OBGYN instructed me not to take any medicines. They left me for hours, and then a nurse came in. He went to administer a bag of medicine. I asked him what it was. He told me if he had time to explain everything to every patient that he would never get his work done. I was appalled as a medical professional.

I tried to drop hints that I knew some things without trying to tell him how to do his job. He ran the bag and left the room. I started to feel sick right away. He came back after while and removed it and threw it in the regular trash, and not the sharps trash. I noticed right away, but he left out so fast I could not say anything. He also left my I. V. dripping on the floor. Disconnected. Royal helped me to the bathroom, and I was sick as a dog. No one came back in the room for the night, until the morning shift change. When I asked what medicine that was, I informed them that I started bleeding. They were very rude and told me my chart showed no medicines administered. Royal and I insisted and explained. As things escalated a head nurse came to calm us all. She listened to me and checked the trash just to ease my "anxiety," but to her surprise she says…"

"Bingo"

As she pulls the improperly discarded bag of medicine out of the trash. They started apologizing immediately. I lost the baby. I was so angry. It put me in a horrible place mentally.

Everything was cool at work until it wasn't. Royal used to come and sit in the car while I worked.

We lived almost an hour away, so he would hang at the mall and chill in the car.

He would faithfully stand outside the door waiting for me to come out. I love how protective of me he is. That freaked some of my coworkers out. They started questioning if I was being abused. He found a job, but the mall overall was not a good fit for us. We moved back with family, but after I got into a fight with a friend of the family we decided to go a different direction. I was having some issues with my mental health during this time. I was feeling suicidal at the time. I was having delusions. Maya Angelou passed away and I had an out of body experience.

I needed to get some help, and be near my family for a while, so we decided to move up north. We decided to move to Connecticut. I was able to get health insurance and medical cannabis was legal. Only one problem, we were homeless. The apartment we originally planned to move to was not livable. We ended up in a homeless shelter. They made us sleep apart because we were not married. We were blessed to meet some great people during that time, that we still speak to. Once we moved out of the shelter and into our new place things got better.

I got to show Royal New York City. I booked as an extra on the set of *Law and Order SVU*. It was the episode about shooting an unarmed black teen boy.

It was perfect timing, in alignment with what was going on in the world news. I pray often for the world. I say RIP to all of those who lost their lives to violence of any kind and those still missing and suffering.

So, back to New York City. My husband is a hip hop music encyclopedia. He was honored to get to see *Ice T* in person. I got to meet him on set, and he was down to earth.

We made friends with some other musicians. We got to collaborate on a track with the Legendary Bass Player *Charlie Karp,* who played with The Legendary *Jimi Hendrix.* Some of the friends we met took us out to a beautiful dinner and gave us a bachelorette and bachelor party. We decided to get married at the justice of peace. My best friend from home decided that if I married Royal, she was no longer my friend. I spoke about not wanting a sister wife at the time. I never said I did not love him and want to figure it out.

We obviously got married! I always knew "that's a good man savannah" Haha! On a serious note, with everything that we have been through, his consistency has kept us strong. He is honest even if it hurts. We have grown so much as a unit. Back to our special day! We got married on a beautiful winter morning. 12.12! I vowed to love Royal and his music for life. He vowed to let me cook and always do the dishes! He has not let me down there ha-ha! It was just him and I, and it was perfect…

A combination of holistic and medical treatments helped me with a lot of my conditions. After the last miscarriage We saw a fertility specialist. She told me that my uterus was tilted in the nicest way possible. Well, technically tilted the wrong way. It did not mean I could not have children; it just may be a challenge. She also in the nicest way possible called me overweight. She technically said I lacked the discipline not to put too much dressing on my salad. I was hurt. I was determined to get healthy and have a baby.

All the fertility stuff put us in a bad place. Royal was ready to find a sister wife. I was no longer interested. It felt like I was being replaced. I could not give him a child. My worst fear was that another woman, who did not care about Royal like I did could show up and bloop she's pregnant. I was dying trying to give him a child. We argued about it often. I would scream and cry and he would calmly hold the same position on how he felt. I could take it or leave it. I decided to leave it…

I went into the bathroom and attempted to commit suicide again. I took more pills this time and drank. I got into the tub. Royal found me and rushed me to the hospital. I can remember coming too and the nurse caring for me had a tattoo on her arm. She explained it was for her brother who committed suicide. He passed away. I felt horrible.

She was so kind and told me she was happy that I was still here. She also told me that Loyal was waiting on me in the lobby. I told her that I did not want to see him. She said that he was really worried about me and saved my life. She told me to give him a chance to make it right. I started balling crying. She hugged me and then got Royal. He came in the room and the look in his eyes I realized that he loved me. They kept me for a few days and then let me go home.

Royal and I decided to move back down south. Right before we left I had a dental appointment for a simple fill. I left with two route canals on the same tooth, but opposite sides. The dentist left the nerve in both of them. I found out when I got to the dentist in NC. They said it could have killed me. I have had issues with dentists since. People laugh at people missing teeth, but you never know how they lost them.

We were happy to be in NC again. We found a place and started our jobs at *Staples*. We still did not have any children; so, we decided to visit my family in NY. My uncle fell ill, and we ended up staying a few months to help. Royal learned how to shovel in a real winter storm! After he was feeling better we received job offers to go to California. We accepted and Royal got accepted into school. He was learning to be a producer.

We drove across country. It was the best experience of my life. We stopped in Atlantic City and got to see *112 & Jon B*. perform. We got to see all of Highway 40 from east to west. It took us a few days to complete the trip. Young and dumb, but adventurous. We did not check the weather. Oh, my goodness, we arrive in Oklahoma's tornado alley. We got there right after the storm left. Everything looked damaged and trees were down. Our next stop was Arizona. That was magical! The skies and the landscape out there is breathtaking. So is Colorado, and Utah. We stopped there on another road trip from California to New York.

We got to Cali, and it was a whole new world. The beaches, the sun, the highways, and traffic. We worked on Sunset Blvd in Hollywood. It was an experience. It was stressful because of our housing situation, but overall, we made the best of being in a new place. The apartment we had in NC last reported our move out wrong, so it caused us not to be able to rent temporarily. We did not let that stop us. We went to Las Vegas and had the time of our lives. We loved the *Flamingo Hotel* the best! We got to see Bow Wow perform and host a pool party. It was a once in a lifetime experience and a blessed time.

The flow of life, the hoods, the food, and the homeless population was different than anywhere we had been. As much as we loved the west coast, we could not keep staying in *Motel 6* and *Extended Stays*.

We decided to move back east. We accepted job transfers to Atlanta. Atlanta was amazing and horrible at the same time. The city overall is beautiful and has a lot of places to see. We went to the *National Center For Civil and Human Rights*. The simulations and overall experience was life changing. I am so grateful for my ancestors and the people who came before me.

When we arrived, we were staying at an extended stay. We found an apartment, and I was so excited. It was gorgeous. Unfortunately, we would not enjoy it long, Royal and I were still up and down. We woke up one morning and it was down. All the way down, or I guess I should say up! He told me in so many words I needed to accept he was not the man for me. I was thrown off because the night before was amazing.

He dropped me off at school and I gave him my wedding rings. I was freaking out wondering whether he would come back. I felt so lost. I logged on my social media to reach out to my home girl. I found a message request from my old side boyfriend. He was congratulating me on getting married, it was a year old. I don't know how I did not see it before then, but I messaged and said thank you. He wrote back and asked how I was. I explained life at the time. He expressed he was newly free after many years. I told him I was in school, giving Atlanta a try. That is where I made my mistake. His page said he was in NY, but he was actually, in Georgia. Twenty minutes away from me. Now he was on the way…

He pulled up to pick me up from school. I went with him to his house. I felt like I was in the twilight zone. I was just married to my man and wanted to spend forever with him, to in the car with my ex. When we got to his house, his mom was there. I was happy to see her, but it all felt like a bad dream.

Him and I went upstairs, and she left to run errands. We talked and caught up. Of course he wanted to have sex. God forbid we just talk and give me a day to air out. I tried to divert the moment by saying I had not waxed. I also shared that I had recently been with my husband. He said he did not care about all of that. He pulled my pants down and I felt like I was in high school again. He got on top of me, and I wanted to believe this was fate. They say if you love something let it go, and if it comes back its yours. How was I in this moment? I looked up and told him that I loved him. He changed positions. I knew then I was nothing to him but sex. It was not fate, but guess what was…

I found out a few weeks to a month after that I was pregnant with our oldest daughter. I remember seeing the test and thinking why now. I prayed for a child for so long. I would have to go through my pregnancy not knowing who the father of my child was. I was married, this was not how all of this was supposed to go. I told both of them the truth. My ex said why was I telling him and they were in the same week. When I told Royal he got out of the car and left on foot, I had to beg him to come back.

Royal is a good man. He told me that she was ours no matter what and that he wanted our family. He told me to keep her, and he would be there for us no matter what. He never missed an appointment. I didn't hear from my ex until I was almost due, he asked to pull up on me I told him get lost. Don t want me now.

We ended up losing our apartment. We were sleeping between our car and hotels. We found a place through a friend of ours from college. We were grateful to get setup, but it was riddled with mold. We had to leave and were out of a bunch of money. We were back to sleeping in the car.

One of Royal's coworkers heard that and offered us a place to stay. We were so thankful because I was 7 months pregnant. We spent the summer with them. I watched his girlfriend's daughter, and they all worked. I drove everyone around, cleaned, and cooked. I was doing classes online. Things were ok until they were not. There was a lot of behaviors that we did not respect or appreciate. We thanked bro, but it was time to go.

We lived at the Motel 6 in Norcross. I woke up and my water broke on the hardwood floor and tile. I went into labor bright and early in the morning. Thank God because we did not get stuck in traffic. We arrived at the hospital, and they were all ready for us. Our doula was amazing.

She did not judge us for living in the hotel. The entire experience was amazing; I had an all-woman staff. They were kind and attentive. Royal was right there the entire time; Baby girl made her appearance 15 hours later. She was perfect. I could not believe I was a mom. We brought her home to the Motel 6 for one night. She slept in between us. I should say Royal and her slept. I sat up all night staring at them. I loved my little family. We moved into an extended stay. We did our best to make it home. After 4 months Royal's dad told us to move back home. He said that we did not need to be in a hotel room. He was right and right on time. The Pandemic hit a month later. We would have been in trouble going from room to room during all of that. We moved back to NC. Royal got a job in highway safety, and I took care of baby girl." Journee says with a smile.

"Journee your story is inspirational. I am proud of both of you for doing what was best for your child. Your family. I am going to use the restroom and then we will continue." Dr. Stone says with a smile exiting the room.

CHAPTER 10

"Pandemic..."

10

Journee and her family were truly blessed to find their new home. It was close to papa and had almost everything they needed. Almost...

"Ok, let's talk about the pandemic and the rest of your pregnancy. The first year of your oldest daughters life, and postpartum. You may begin when you're ready." Dr. Stone says eagerly with her pen and notebook ready.

"The Pandemic. Oooowee, that was a time for sure and not in a good way. I know now we are truly blessed. We had a beautiful townhouse. It felt like everything was coming together. but it was tough. Mainly, our marriage. Royal and I were still in a distant space. Not talking much, he was barely interacting with me. It made it worse, because of all times, it was a pandemic. I could not go out and get a break. He was not caring for me that pregnancy, the way he had the first one. Him not speaking to me was hurting me so badly, and him working long hours far away gave me terrible anxiety. I prayed for his safety on the road daily.

I was taking care of my oldest while pregnant and dealing with horrible sciatica. I knew by this point I lost one of the babies. It hurt to realize I would not be a twin mom, although everyone always asks are the girls twins. They are both so smart and funny, they even know to say in unison, were 13 months apart ha-ha! Babygirl was so smart and inquisitive from day one. She was walking by 9 months, feeding herself, and getting into everything by a year old. I did my best to keep up and not let her see me emotionally breaking down. I feel horrible knowing now that when I closed the door to cry, little mama was feeling it inside.

We found a doula through social media. It did not go as well as our first experience in Georgia. I thought I was in labor. We drove all the way to the hospital. She met us there. When they told me I was not in labor, she flipped and caused this whole scene. She made the hospital feel I was being difficult and almost got me banned. It was way to much to be dealing with while pregnant, so we parted ways with her.

We celebrated Babygirl turning a year. I made her a huge Paddington Bear cake, and papa came. My mom, grandma, and uncle facetimed us! My granddad called us. My sister and aunts text us. It was a beautiful celebration of her life, but also the celebration of her graduating to big sis!

Things started to look up, so I thought. Royal seemed to be in a better mood. We were not having sex, but we at least were laughing together again. I learned quickly that I was not the reason for his joy. I was eating a bowl of cereal one day, watching tv, and he text me from taking out the trash that he wanted to talk to me about something. He said it was nothing bad, so I got excited. He came in and let me know that he had been talking to someone. A girl he knew from high school. He was telling me because he felt things were going from cordial to possibly something more. When I asked to see the messages, he could not show me, because it was *Snapchat*. That made it worse, I had no idea what was being said between them.

I felt like I got hit by a bus. I felt so stupid, why did I stay? Why would he tell me he still wanted our family to have me here to do this? I asked him to be real with me and explain where this was going. He said he was not sure, but he was willing to explore it. I told him I did not think it was a good idea, or timing to include someone in our relationship. We weren't in a good place, why invite someone to be miserable with us. I learned I wasn't invited. For the first time in our relationship, it was no longer about me being a bisexual woman. It was about him being a polygamous man. This was all news to me. I did my best to breathe and rub my stomach as he was speaking. I always respect his honesty, but my heart was breaking. I wanted to die. He went on to explain that he would be willing to consider having more than one wife, if she was not interested in women to join our marriage. I did not want a sister wife at the time, so for him to change lanes, I was thrown off. I told him I needed time to process and maybe after I gave birth in a few days.

He proceeded to message her anyway to see how she felt. To add insult to injury she does not like women and technically rejected me out of the equation and invited him over to help her move furniture. This woman knew about me, and he spoke to her about my medical conditions, and she still pushed. He was prepared to pack me up at 8 months pregnant and our one year old child, to go and help her, because he is still a gentleman. When he told her that we were coming too, she said she did not need his help anymore. Then put up shady subliminal messages online. I was even more mad, because I had to watch him go from being genuine with someone he thought he knew. He owned his truths with me, and she played in our face. I had to watch him go through the feelings caused by another woman. I was over all of it.

I woke up that Sunday knowing I was in labor. I had Royal take me to the hospital, and Papa had Babygirl. We were sad that no one could come to the hospital because of covid, but we were excited to meet our Babygirl. The hospital was almost two hours away. We got there. They checked on her and sent me home.

They said I was not in labor. We drove all the way back home.

By 2:30 am I woke up in excruciating pains and constant contractions. It felt like she was coming out. But my water had not broken. I am so glad that I trusted my instincts and we headed to the hospital. We had to stop at the *Sheetz* to get gas. The way I was moaning, other customers were all staring. I could barely breathe. Then, my water burst all in the seat. I knew she was coming. We got to the hospital at 5 am. They quickly gave me an epidural and said it was time to push. By 5:25 am Monday morning she burst her way into the world! It was so beautiful to hear her cry, the mask and all the protocols were worth that moment.

Unfortunately, the moment took a turn quickly. The nurse said…"

"oops!"

"Royal and I both said what's oops. She explained that while pulling on my umbilical cord, she accidentally ripped it from the placenta. I do not know why she was pulling, and it expels on its own. They tried to get it out. They were arm deep inside of me trying to get it out, but said my cervix was rapidly closing. They rushed me to the back for an emergency procedure. The hospital appointed doula was told she could not come with me. So, I went to the back, and my husband was left with a new baby.

I was so thankful to see when I came back she was on his chest sleeping peacefully. He had his shirt off, doing skin to skin. He had his shoulders, and her draped with a blanket. They looked perfect to me. I fell in love with him all over again.

We went home the next day. Hubs does not do well in hospitals, so he was packed before the ink on the discharge paperwork dried. We headed home to relive Papa and officially become a family of 4. Babygirl looked at her sister and then hit her. We had to teach her to be gentle, and they have been attached at the hip since.

Being new parents and adjusting to having two children under the age of two, was a journey and a challenge. God is good! Royal and I were still in a distant space intimately. We would barley cuddle or make love. We were watching a show called *Monogamy* one night. He had been resistant to watch it with me, because it showed a lot of drama and infidelity. I thought it was an interesting show because it show different dynamics of different couples. There was a scene that changed our relationship forever. The female character was masturbating in front of the male character. They just finished having sex. He joked that he wasn't enough for her, but she started speaking her traumatic experiences aloud. She proceeded to want him to have sex with her aggressively. It introduced us to a "dark side" of role play, but I was grateful that we were connecting again...

Being alone with a one year old and a newborn during a pandemic was not easy at all.

I loved being a mother, but my mind was turning on me. I am thankful for my therapist at the time. Thank God for technology, I was able to have virtual appointments live from the house. I was able to talk to her about almost everything. She represented balance for me and was a great voice of reason for me during that time. She witnessed some of the challenges I was facing with the babies by myself. One day I had the youngest in my arms crying for hours, I was learning then she wasn't feeling well. Breastfeeding was not going as well as my first pregnancy. Having had a reduction, it was hit or miss. I was thankful to produce any milk. She was having yellow dust in her diaper and her stomach clearly hurt her. I learned through trial and error that she was sensitive to the formula. The dairy free purple formula worked best for her. Once we found that she felt so much better. My little sister sent me food on *DoorDash*. I was having horrible postpartum. The thoughts I was having were not safe, and very hard to deal with. I am so thankful for my village.

We were adjusting as best as we could. Royal was loving his job, but things started to change. They accused him of stealing tools. He would never. They found them later and apologized, but it broke the trust he built with them. He resigned not long after, he did not want to leave room for them to tarnish his record or worse. It really devastated him. He had so much pride in providing for his family. I tried my best to heal his ego, but I know now it is something a man has to work through on his own.

It really put us deeper into a depression and distant space. Royal said he felt trapped; it was too small. In my opinion, It was perfect for us, but I was leaning into our relationship at the time. I learned later he was leaning out.

Things with the girls growth and health had been consistent. We got sick as a family twice during the pandemic, but overall, we were truly blessed. Our youngest baby girl took a turn we never saw coming. I noticed she was slower to do some of the functions and meet milestones, but she was still making great progress. She did not walk or eat solids well yet, but she was such a happy baby when she was not hurting. We got her into therapy. She got thrush in her mouth. After that she stopped eating. Eventually she was not urinating. Her hair was falling out and her color was leaving her skin. She was a year, so they stopped the special WIC formula. They kept telling us she was ok, but we took her for a second opinion. She ended up hospitalized. They placed a g tube, and she started to thrive. It was one hell of an experience. Royal and I would swap out once a day. I would spend night with our oldest, and he would sleep at the hospital. Then, I would be there during the day, and he get rest and chill with our oldest. We never left her alone. We did not want her to feel we left her. She was so happy the day she came home. She had to have teeth removed due to the malnutrition, but she started to do better.

I started going back to school. I completed a Nursing program and started working homecare. I learned very quickly that my body, post babies was not the same. My back could not do what it once did. I resigned from my position and closed the chapter of my life working in healthcare. It all worked out, because it was a lot for Royal at the house with two infants and one on a feeding machine and schedule. I needed to be with them.

By this point with Royal not working, bills were catching up fast and rent was due. I accepted a job from our family friend. I worked from home. I gathered and gave resources and information to people in need. It gave me a purpose during the pandemic. I could not go back to the medical field physically, so I also started *Instacart* delivering. I did it in the height of the pandemic. I accepted orders of a certain size and weight limit. I was driving all over North Carolina. From Raleigh to Fayetteville, From Pittsboro, to Fuquay Varina. The world was so different at that time. The masks, the gloves, the signs, the empty stores, it felt like an apocalypse movie.

I had another moment that felt like a movie, but a horror film. I was driving home from Walmart on the backroad one day. I saw a truck with wheels jacked up in the distance behind me. It was speeding up, so I was prepared for them to go around me. However, they did not pass me. They sped up and stayed so close I feared they would hit me. I waited for a safe opening, and I pulled into a ditch.

When they passed me I got back onto the road. I was on facetime with Royal, so I turned the phone to show the truck going down the road. They saw me and started hanging machetes out the window. They kept braking to make me hit them. I crossed a double lane to pass them and another car. I thought I lost them turning rapidly down my side street, but they turned after me. I pulled in front the house parallel. I hopped out with my gun drawn and pointed in the air. I told them to get from in front of my house, or I would shoot. They took out their phones and took pictures and videos of me. They kept circling the neighborhood.

We called the police and Papa to come. He got there almost as fast as them. The officer put them in handcuffs. They said I was lying, and we threatened them, but the machetes were in the car. The officer said the same as I heard with being attacked by my ex. These people were out front of my home, and yet still, I would have to be arrested as well since he said we threatened him. The officer asked what I wanted to do. I thought hard and decided not to press charges. I could not leave my babies. I asked for his name and address since he had mine. Come to find out he lived on the street behind us, hence why he was so comfortable to swing that corner like I did.

I had horrible anxiety after that. I would be up all ours of the night looking out the windows and watching the cameras. I was losing it. I hated leaving the house, but I had to keep going.

It was not all bad. God always has a way of showing you that he is right on time. The best tip I received while doing *Instacart* was from a house on one of my favorite backroads, it was also one of the biggest orders I have ever accepted. We needed the money.

I was still actively miscarrying. I knew the doctors said the baby would expel on its own. That started to happen in *Sheetz* bathroom, in the middle on their order. I had a car full of groceries. I cried and did not want to stand up. The toilet was going to flush my baby away. I finally stood up. I cleaned myself up as best I could. I filled my pants with paper towels. I washed my face and hands in the sink. I stood at the drier zoned out for a moment and then my phone notification went off.

I was late delivering the order. I rushed there to deliver their order because I could not get a bad review. That would drop my rating, meaning less money for harder jobs. I told the app it was my last order. I was short by my goal by $10. Normally I would grab one last one and head home. I could barely walk. I was sweating profusely in the heat. The house was a double wide trailer set on acres of land.

There was a white man in the distance coming towards me. I was immediately terrified. I started grabbing the groceries so fast, he kept coming across the field like *Jeepers Creepers*. I am about to throw up by this point. He spoke as he walked up to the car and startled me. I quickly nodded hello and kept grabbing groceries.

The car seemed like it was still full every time I came back to it. He started helping me get backs out the trunk. I told him it was ok and not his job. He told me he did not mind. Finally, he pulled out his wallet and handed me a $50 bill. I immediately told him no; that I was late and apologized again. He told me that I did an amazing job, and he wanted me to go home. He then told me I had blood on my pants. I was mortified. I know he probably assumed I had my period. If only he knew how much his generosity and care meant in that moment. I thanked him and headed out. As I did, a child got off the school bus. When I saw the child I realized I judged that man. The same way I would not have wanted him to judge me, or someone judge my husband immediately. He added an extra $25 tip on the app as well and left a great review. Over time that trailer became a beautiful home on a farm. I think of them when I pass by.

Our cars transmission started to break down on us. I was falling apart. We barely had money, and the car was the only way to make more. I met an amazing Female Mechanic through AAA. She helped me and has truly been God sent. I still talk to and cater some of her events to this day!

During this time, we got word from our brother. He had a court date, and he needed us there. We got on the road and arrived right at the courthouse on time. He was being accused of raping his girlfriend's daughter. She found out he cheated and put the story together. I testified in a sweatsuit, straight off the road. I was so sad to see my brother sitting there. I spoke honestly and fairly to everyone involved. I was free to go, but my brother wasn't. Despite no evidence, and her signed affidavit saying that he was innocent, he was sentenced to life. It crushed us all. I lost a baby stressing over this situation. He lost the right to be with his kids. It hurt to watch someone's life be ruined. We are trying to figure out how to help him.

I started applying for jobs and looking for new places to live. We needed a fresh start." Journee says with tears in her eyes.

"Wow. I do not normally do this, but may I give you a hug? If not I completely understand as well." Dr. Stone says genuinely.

"Yes, that would be ok." Journee says embracing the hug.

246

CHAPTER 11

"New Job = New Life…"

11

"Ok, let's move on to the last section of your timeline. The incident that led to your incarceration, your time in jail, and what you have done since. I will gather all of my notes and produce a plan that we will go over together. You may begin when you are ready." Dr. Stone says warmly.

"Well, I got a job at *GameStop* First. I thought it was the perfect fit. We are a gaming household. I loved the store and the manager. I unfortunately decided to resign from the offer and not take the position. They needed me to work multiple stores in more than one location, with the girls and baby girl's condition I could not accept the job.

I got hired next at the new *Dollar General*. I had a resume to qualify to be a store manager, but they offered me sales associate. I thought it was a "work your way up" position, so I was willing to accept. Then, they told me the pay.

I found a job at a call center. The pay was good and the benefits for school was even better. I started working there in January. I lived two hours away when I started. Baby girl still had her feeding tube. Royal was managing his PTSD as best as possible We were arguing often. The girls were not potty trained yet, so it was a lot. We started teaching them, but it was a process.

The job was going well. I enjoyed what I was doing. I was attending online classes for WGU. I was majoring in Network Security and IT Management. I was doing well in my classes, but when I would check in on home, it was not going well. Royal was overwhelmed. I told my job I needed to find a place closer, or I would have to resign. They granted me a 30 day leave to move. I was so thankful. We found a place and moved closer to the job.

I thought things were falling into place finally. I was working, I had my business still, and the girls were doing so good. Royal and I were still not seeing eye to eye. Things were spiraling out fast for me. I was not getting much sleep. I was taking herbs just to keep up. Things did not look like they were getting better. I got a call from Royal, that the neighbors called the police. They said the girls were screaming. Royal and I did not see eye to eye on spanking, because I did not get them growing up and he did. I did not ever think it was to the point of calling the police. I learned later they just have something against us. They have called multiple times and Thank God the officers leave each time because there is no disturbance.

Things were not getting any better and mentally I was breaking down. I realized that just because I learned to master a smile, that I still had to be real with myself and those I trust. If I had done so, this may have been avoided.

The job environment went from fun and productive to stressful. I was having chest pains, popping *Bayer Aspirin* like they were *Reese's pieces*. I was being bullied at the job. People had opinions on our domestic situation and some joked about it. My manager was delaying my tuition reimbursement, so I was falling behind financially.

That same manager joked that a tool for our job should be my best friend. She went on to say laughing…"

"As a matter of fact, it should be your new husband. Oh wait, too soon?"

"In front of her, I had a male manager tell me that everything would be ok, I just need a little Capricorn in my life. Then, he gestured that he was stroking something. That is the same manager that told me I did not have to come back, but then did not speak up to say he said it. I tried my best to be kind to people. It seemed like the nicer I was, the meaner they were. I was asked to make cupcakes for our graduation ceremony. My manager waited until we were back at our desk packing to leave. She handed me the cupcakes I made, and they were all flipped upside down. All of them. I have never cried so much at a job in my life.

I talked to my family in NY and asked if I could come stay with the girls for a little while. Give Royal and I some space to heal. They said yes. I was able to get my job on board. They agreed that I could transfer. I was so happy, because that meant I could keep taking my classes and would have income to find a place. Royal and I came to an understanding. The girls and I packed up to leave. It was hard to say goodbye too him and the girls knew something was going on. My oldest cried out for her daddy most of the ride.

When I got to NY and got settled, the job said I had to come back. They said I had to finish my last few weeks there and then transfer. Leaving my kids was not what my mom and I agreed on. She understood, but that arrangement was expiring fast. I started driving back and forth between NY and NC once a week. By the end of the month, I was exhausted.

My last trip in NY I got into it with my mom. I expressed I was not doing well mentally. I left with the girls in the middle of the night on no sleep. I was in a dark place. I was hearing voices at this point. It felt like someone was sitting in the passenger seat. They told me to shoot both girls and drive off the road. It is truly a miracle that I made it down the road. I had enough money to feed them. I survived on prayer.

I dropped the girls to the house and then I left to call the job. I tried to explain to them that I was in crisis. I told them my mind was telling me to harm the girls: I was worried Royal would hurt them. I needed help. We needed help. They said be there by noon or I was terminated and hung up. All I could think, I fed people, I was on time, I gave people rides, and I did a damn good job with our customers. I felt discarded and worthless. This was the lowest I have ever been in my life.

I called my family to say my goodbyes. I was prepared to shoot myself. Then my mind said that I should do it in front of HR. They enjoyed my pain I thought. I pulled in the job. My home girl arrived as I was walking up to the building. She screamed for me, but I was too far gone.

I shot the glass door. I cleared the glass and entered the building. I went straight to HR and asked to speak to the rep from the phone. She stood up. I walked towards her. I let her know I would not hurt her. I told her that I needed help. No one was taking me seriously. My mind was racing a million miles a minute. I was breathing heavily.

She called my mom. My mom pleaded for me not to hurt anyone or myself. After everything we have been through, she saved my life. She said exactly what I needed to hear. She was there for me and our family through it all in ways that I could have never imagined. I am working to give her the world now, but in that moment, I told her to get the girls.

I prepared to be killed by the police. I went outside. I don't know how my legs were moving. I could barely hear the sounds around me. I cut my face on glass going back out and didn't realize it.

I figured it out because Royal was there now. He pulled up with the girls. I hugged him and I told him to get away from me because I thought the police would kill me.

I surrendered, and as he was pulling out with the girls they pulled him over. They surrounded the truck and drew weapons on them. I was screaming my children were in there. They slammed Royal and arrested him. He was there to help me, and they arrested him. As they were driving me away and putting him in the car, he yelled out that he still loved me. It gave me chills. I was numb. For the first time in my life, in a stressful situation, I was not crying.

I thank God our children went with family. I was so out of it I did not recognize people I knew. The Detective said something to me before they took me to the jail. He asked me did I have faith. I told him yes. He said it was all going to be bad, but if I stood on faith, in the end I would be ok. I cried so hard on the ride to jail, but he was right. I prayed and wiped my tears. Royal was released from jail, but they put me on a million dollar bond. I was not going anywhere. Jail was a horrible but an enlightening experience. I was sexually harassed before I got my uniform. A guy booking out asked me if I wanted to,"

"Taste some dick before I go away, since it will be a while."

"I ignored him and watched myself being talked about on the news. It was a horrible feeling. I had to be strong, but I was dying inside. I was on my cycle and told I could not have my clothes: I was on suicide watch. I had to beg to keep my pull up.

I learned how strong I truly am. I learned the power of prayer and reading your word. I found Psalms 142:7 "bring me out of prison, so I may give praise to his name." I recited that to myself every day. I prayed with other inmates as well. That was the most powerful of everything I witnessed.

Hearing my families voices on the phone was a blessing and torture at the same time. I am grateful for technology. The tablets are a lifesaver. I was able to take classes and watch some great motivational shows. There was a series dedicated to us during the pandemic. There was no in person visits anymore. I learned so many peoples stories. I learned you never know what someone has been through. I was able to reset my love for reading and writing. I read 35 books while I was there. The one that stands out most is *The Body Keeps The Score.* by *Bessel A., Van Der Kolk.* The therapist gave it to me. Hearing the stories of some of the women in there, changed me for life.

I had to go home on ankle monitoring while I awaited sentencing.

That was a humbling experience. I had a strict curfew. That was not hard to adhere to, but not being able to go as I pleased was difficult. To escape I would sit in my car and listen to music. I started recording videos of me singing and freestyling in the car, because you could not see my ankle. I still do them, but now per request! It saved my life and helped me heal. After 120 days I was able to be with my family again. I was placed on probation.

I am honored that my prior manager came to the court hearing. She spoke directly to me. She apologized and said I was trying to tell her something, but she did not listen. I cried so hard. My hands left sweat prints on the table as I awaited sentencing. I would not wish that on anyone. You are waiting to learn your fate. If you will be given another chance or is life as you know it over. I am truly grateful to be free. My Lawyer was a blessing as well. He helped me through the hardest time in my life. I am grateful that I was clearly surrounded by people with real faith and angels. I want to do, whatever I have to do, in order to give my babies, the best life possible. Full of love and my presence." Journee says with tears in her eyes.

CHAPTER 12

"Healing Journee…"

12

"Journee, I mean this with all of me, you are phenomenal!" Dr. Stone says, reaching out to hold Journee's hands.

"You are one of the strongest people I have ever met. I get chills when I hear stories like yours. Not because of all the trauma, but how you overcame it. Time after time you pushed to keep going. You may have stumbled, and it looked like giving up, but we know now you were just getting going!

I would like to go over the treatment plan that I feel will best fit your needs. We are a long-term program, so we are here to support in all areas of life. I am recommending 5 weeks of intensive childhood trauma therapy and healing exercises. 5 weeks of the sexual abuse and trafficking therapy and healing program. 5 weeks of postpartum/ post loss of pregnancy therapy, and 5 weeks of spouse attended marriage support sessions. Lastly, 5 weeks of skills for coping with fear, sadness, and anger.

I would also like you to do a 7-day detox and spiritual reset. Once you complete that I am starting you on a medication regimen. I see you took Adderall before. I think that *Wellbutrin* and *Zoloft* will be a better fit. Let's start there on a low dose of both. I have seen great results for patients with similar symptoms as you. In the matrix its red or blue pill, but in real life you get both to help you conquer the world!

I want you to bring the girls and hubs to a couple of sessions as well. I want to always make sure we maintain their little mental and emotional health as well. Your husband is locked in with the VA hospital, so that is great for a lot of resources.

Lastly, I want you to attend the monthly vision board and women's group meetings. It is always great to heal through watching others heal as well. I am so proud of you and all that you plan to accomplish. I believe in your music and your message. You are going to help so many people. That is a beautiful purpose to have. The book that I want you to read is *The Alchemist* by *Paulo Coelho*. This is your copy. I am sure that I will have other titles to help as you go on your journey: but Journee, I look forward to watching you heal, evolve, and continue to grow! Your first assignment is to write what you would tell your younger self looking back. We can do this first one together. I want to hear what you would say…" Dr. Stone says with tears of joy in her eyes and optimism.

"First, I would like to thank you for recording all of what I remember. Now, If I could tell my younger self anything, I would tell her that I love her and thank you. I would tell her to stay focused and keep God first always. Like my father in law says…"

"If you're going to worry why pray, and if you're going to pray why worry!"

"I would tell her don't be in a hurry to grow up. Enjoy each phase of life and take your time. I would tell her not to get distracted. Know that fun will always be there, but you won't be, if you waste the one life that God gave you. Learn who you really are and master that. Wait for what you really want. If you start something finish it, no matter how challenging.

If you make a promise, don't break that. You may not get the opportunity to do things over, so be intentional in each moment and teach that to your children. Be honest and have integrity. No is a complete sentence. You do not have to do anything that you don't want to. I would tell her If she is dealing with someone, wrap up completely and then pursue someone else. Taking that time in between can help you heal and choose your next partner wisely. I'd tell her that she can achieve anything she puts her mind to. Avoid people that tell you that you can't do something.

Know that every decision you make will stay with you for life; especially online, so be careful. You do not have to live in fear, just be aware of your surroundings. Don't let people take your kindness for weakness. Avoid people that are not feeling your vibe, or you irritate their spirit with your joy. I would say not to be so trusting, and that no one owes you anything but borrowed money. They do not have to respect you, even if you respect them. Respect your parents and elders Respect yourself and never accept any form of disrespect; from anyone.

Speaking of disrespect, the basketball player that raped me, had the audacity to put a post on social media that addressed the incident. He said there are two sides, to every story, and the truth. Go write a book about it because nobody cares! I said to myself, I just might do that.

I appreciate this conversation today. I feel heard and seen. I no longer feel like I am running from the past. Everyone makes mistakes, but it is a bad habit if you don't change to be better. I love that Royal and I have been seeking therapy. I owned up to all of my past and my mistakes. He apologized and took accountability for a lot as well. It feels so good to live in our purpose. Yoga and meditation has really been balancing things in our household. I am so grateful for him. He has said some things to me that, I know God was speaking through him. I am focused on us and continuing to heal our family.

The girls are amazing. We are truly blessed. I look forward to exploring what hobbies that the girls may be interested in. Their dad signed them up for self-defense. He said they can do whatever, as long as they can protect themselves. Haha! I agree though.

Thank you Alesha, for dedicating your life to helping others. As an artist I try to do the same.

I LOVE music! Our official song is *Saturday Love* by *Cherrelle and Alexander O'Neal*. The girls literally learned the days of the week because of that song. Haha! Speaking of music, who is your favorite artist?" Journee says bright eyed, and curious as to what Dr. Stone's response will be…

CHAPTER 13

"No More Rain (In This Cloud)"

13

"I am a huge Angie Stone fan. I was incredibly sad to hear the news of her passing. I also believe you can do anything you put your mind to. If you believe it. You can achieve it!" Dr. Stone says enthusiastically.

"My mom always says that!. *"No More Rain (In This Cloud)* is one of the songs I play when I need a pick me up, & *Donnie McClurkin's* song *Stand.*" Journee says cheerfully. **(Bing)** Journee's phone notification goes off.

"I'm sorry, enough about me for today. Take your call. I'll see you at our next session! Dr. Stone says sincerely. Journee is still staring at her phone.

"What's wrong Journee? You look like you just seen a ghost." Dr. Stone says with a bit of nervous laughter herself.

"It is not a phone call. It is a notification from the DNA company. It says they found a close family match from my dad's side." Journee says looking up at Dr. Stone puzzled, but optimistic.

"Wow. This is what you prayed for. Just take your time. When you are ready, open it or open it at our next session. Journee, Just breathe..." Dr. Stone says calmy...

The End

Published by

J.UNIQUE

PUBLISHED IT

Journee's Jail Book List

1. Janet Evanovich- Three to Get Deadly
2. Jonathan Kellerman- A Cold Heart
3. Sue Grafton- N is for Noose
4. Sue Grafton- S is for Silence
5. Janet Evanovich- Ten Big Ones
6. Janet Evanovich- Fearless 14, Finger lickin 15
7. Janet Evanovich- The Heist
8. Terri Blackstock- Double Minds
9. Janet Evanovich- Full Speed
10. Janet Evanovich- Love Overboard
11. Bessel Van Der Kolk- The Body Keeps Score
12. Debbie Macomber- 311 Pelican Court
13. Debbie Macomber- 92 Pacific Boulevard
14. Maria Stemple- Where'd you go Bernadette
15. Patricia Cornwell- Depraved Heart
16. Debbie Macomber- 1105 Yakima Street
17. Debbie Macomber- 1225 Christmas Tree Lane
18. Jonathan Kellerman- Obsession
19. The ESV Study Bible
20. James Patterson- Violets are Blue
21. Jonathan Kellerman- Time Bomb
22. Lisa Jackson- Without Mercy
23. Janet Evanovich- Hard 8
24. Lisa Jackson- Twice Kissed
25. Janet Evanovich- Tricky Twenty- two
26. Janet Evanovich- Hardcore Twenty- Four
27. Nicole Trope- The Family Across the Street
28. Nicholos Sparks- Dear John
29. Janet Evanovich- Takedown Twenty
30. Janet Evanovich- Four to Score
31. Janet Evanovich- Seven Up
32. Ashley Antoinette- Ethic IV
33. Janet Evanovich- Twisted Twenty- Six
34. Janet Evanovich- Tantalizing Twenty Seven
35. Tabitha Brown- Feeding the Soul (Because it's my business)

New Books Coming From J Unique
Published It:

1. The Skin I'm In (Children's book): June 19th, 2025
2. Dream. Publish. Repeat! (Self-Publishing Guide): June 27th, 2025
3. Emelyn and Londyn go on an Adventure (children's book): August 18th, 2025
4. A Familiar Walk With A Stranger- (Suspense Novel): October 2025
5. The "Home Cook Cookbook": November 2025
6. The Entrepreneur's Guide (business guide): November 29th, 2025

Scan the QRC CODE below to Join Our FREE mailing list to be able to receive updates on new releases, giveaways, events, and more!

Here is a Recipe

Sneak Preview

From

J Unique Published It

"The Home Cook Cookbook"

coming Nov 2025!

Easy Shepard's Pie

Prep: Clean surface, and wash hands. Lay out all supplies. Pre peel and dice veggies. Set your vibe with music and enjoy the process!

Grocery list: Payment options: All tenders will work based on location. Some locations WIC friendly (vegetables only)

1. 2 pounds of ground beef or *substitute
2. 2 8 oz bags of frozen peas and carrots
3. One onion (diced) One pepper (diced)
4. 5-pound bag of potatoes (peeled)
5. One cup of Milk or Sour Cream. (or ½ c & ½c)
6. One bag of sharp cheese
7. One large can of tomato paste
8. One and a half sticks of butter (melt one stick)
9. Spices of choice.

Recipe Step by Step:

1. Pre Heat oven to 375
2. Peel your potatoes and boil them in water with until soft. Drain them & carefully whip until smooth. Add spices & melted butter, then wet ingredient of choice.
3. Sauté in half stick of butter, your peppers and onions and set them to the side. Brown your ground beef and season to taste.
4. Add the onions and peppers, the tomato paste, and peas and carrots.
5. In a baking dish pour your meat mixture and top with cheese.
6. Put your slightly cooled mashed potatoes in a **Piping Bag**, pipe them over the top of the cheese.
7. Bake on 375 for 30 minutes or until the mashed potatoes are lightly browned on top.
8. Let rest for 5 minutes and serve with *Martha White* muffins. Enjoy!

I signed this page for everyone who
reads this book!

Jazzlyn Unique Ingram

Bring this to any event and I will
sign here for you personally!